Finding the way Home

ROSELIN CASANOVA

FINDING THE WAY HOME

iUniverse books may be ordered through booksellers or by contacting:

iUniverse
1663 Liberty Drive
Bloomington, IN 47403
www.iuniverse.com
1-800-Authors (1-800-288-4677)

ISBN: 978-1-5320-1384-3 (sc)
ISBN: 978-1-5320-1383-6 (e)

Library of Congress Control Number: 2017901150

Print information available on the last page.

iUniverse rev. date: 01/28/2017

Special Thanks

First, I would like to thank God, as my guide in every step of my earthly journey, for helping me to achieve this goal of completing my first book. I would also like to thank all those people who, in one way or another, are participants and even protagonists of the experiences exposed in these pages. Thanks to my spiritual guides for leading me to along pathway of light, culture, and wisdom. And thanks to you, dear reader, for dedicating part of your precious time to reading my story and perhaps sharing moments described throughout the book, and for motivating me to keep cultivating the art of writing in this world, with several approaches to the everyday life and the spiritual life.

FOREWORD

Finding the Way Home is the story of a young woman's struggle to accomplish her life's purpose. The story is developed in a cross talk between reason and intuition, where intangible feelings such as love, faith, hope, and happiness are constantly judged by the social environment of society. Along her journey, she learns to trust and act upon the guidance of her internal voice and external spiritual supporters to help others in their journeys and finish what brought her back to Earth in the first place. Past life experiences present themselves to her so she can find answers and explanations for the feelings and emotions that were bringing her down into a state of confusion and uncertainty. The main story is accompanied by fascinating reflections, which will leave you not only with valuable messages but also with questions that perhaps everyone must ask themselves.

Rochy

CHAPTER 1

The Beginning

I HAD A HAPPY CHILDHOOD. Ever since I was a young girl, I enjoyed all the material comforts and affection of the people around me. My dresses and my personal hygiene were impeccable, just like a fairy tale princess. My family was used to celebrating many birthdays and important occasions in extravagant fashion, so I was often attired in elegant dresses. My parents always made sure that I wore the best brands: high-quality clothes made by local and national designers. My mother knew how to choose the best colors and designs for each occasion.

I was never alone. I always had somebody taking care of me: listening to me; bathing, dressing, and pampering me. When my parents were busy, as they often were, I was cared for by my Nanny. Tata was the affectionate nickname that my siblings and I gave to our beloved Nanny. The bathroom was the place that I liked the most because I could talk to Tata while she was bathing me. Somehow, I felt that it was my responsibility to keep her entertained so she would enjoy the bathroom as much as I did.

Ever since I was very young, I was extremely afraid of the dark. At night, when my light was turned off before bed, my heart would race, and my mind would start producing terrible images. My imagination had no limits. My heart would beat faster and faster with every thought. Then, my body trembling, I would break out in a cold sweat. When I couldn't take it anymore, I'd leap from my bed and run to turn on the light. Everything disappeared with just the click of the switch. Little by little, my heartbeat would slow down until it regained complete peace and I could go back to sleep.

Back then, I didn't know why I was afraid of the dark and my siblings weren't. That weakness really annoyed me. Together with my cousins and sister, I tried to overcome this inexplicable fear. We'd do exercises in the morning, afternoon, and night. They would keep me company while I was sitting in front of the TV. Sitting behind me, where I couldn't see them, they would silently leave one by one until I was alone in the room. I don't know how, but once I was alone, even though I had no way of knowing because I was forbidden to turn around, I suddenly started to feel bad. I would panic and scream: "come!" Each time we did this exercise, I screamed when left alone. Somehow, I knew when there was no physical company around me.

Because of my fear, I'd grown accustomed to falling asleep in the company of someone throughout my childhood. My nanny was my preferred companion; she'd keep me company until I fell asleep. Still, on most occasions, I'd wake up in the middle of the night, get out of bed frightened and fearful, and run across the hall to my nanny's bedroom. I'd crawl up onto her bed and whisper in her ear:

"Tata, I'm scared. Come to sleep with me."

Sometimes she looked tired and sleepy, but this didn't stop her from getting out of bed to take me to my room, tuck me into my bed again, and then lie down next to me and hold me to protect me until I fell asleep again. Her company kept all the fears that tormented me at bay.

My parents decided to install a small nightlight in my room and my fears diminished a little. But still, I needed Tata's company.

Each time I went to her room at night to get her, I'd see and hear strange things. Doorknobs moved as though there was somebody turning them, even when I knew that there was nobody there. Those experiences reinforced my fears. I would get a feeling like something was surrounding and agitating me so much that I even had trouble breathing.

My attachment to my nanny was very strong. She was virtually everything to me. My affinity for her would cause me to worry about something happening to her, causing me constant nightmares. In most of my nightmares, my nanny died in some way, causing my fear of losing her to grow over the years. I decided to tell her but, attempting to soothe me, she just said, "That means that God will give me more life. Don't worry, I'll be at your side to see you turn into a woman, and I'll be able to witness your children growing up."

I always believed everything she told me.

The nightmares continued. And, although I felt bad at the moment, I remembered her words and began to feel like I could go on.

Tata was a very sickly person. She had chronic diseases, and that's why she frequently looked sick and frail. Several times, I saw my mother take Tata in the car to the hospital. I always made sure to remember her words in moments like those, to avoid crying and to prevent despair from surrounding me. The house looked pale and charmless when she wasn't in it.

I loved my Nanny's strong character. She was very funny when she got angry: she'd frown and start saying words that were specific to her region with a tone of annoyance. But I knew she couldn't stay angry with me for long.

I felt very lucky to have her. During each of my childhood illnesses, she was always there by my side, pleasing me, serving me, making all my favorite dishes. I still remember the songs she'd sing to me with every fiber of my heart.

I was very lazy, so getting out of bed at six in the morning to go to school was like a punishment. My nanny lessened the trauma when she entered my room singing:

"Señora Bonita ..."

By the light of the small lamp, she looked for my clothes in the drawers, while repeating the song over and over. She'd help me get dressed and awake enough to get on with my day. Her patience was impressive and her love was unconditional.

Growing up was a battle for me. I resisted each stage of development. Even during puberty, I'd suck a pacifier at night and drink from a baby bottle to go sleep. I had the female version of the Peter Pan Syndrome; I refused to grow up.

I had a very restless and creative mind. I used to play alone with my imaginary friends. I created movies, short films, TV series, soap operas ... and I played a different role in each of them.

Not everything was sunshine and rainbows. There were comforts, affection, and attention, but, there was also violence and verbal abuse from my father. Even though his behavior was directed at my mother, siblings, and sometimes relatives and friends, I was still affected. I felt deep sadness when these things happened. Many times, I had to comfort the affected people. I didn't judge my father, but I didn't understand why he did what he did.

When my father grew angry, his face would become totally disfigured; he would explode in a rage and become unrecognizable. Looking into his hollow eyes, I could see that my father was no longer there. Something told me that whatever had taken over him wasn't good, but beyond that, I didn't know how to describe the destructive demons behind his stare.

My childhood passed quickly when I was having fun playing sports such as soccer, basketball, and baseball. I loved hanging out and playing with the boys. This made growing into a young lady more difficult for me to accept. My developing breasts hurt very much if they got chafed or bumped in the struggle for the ball. And, because my physical abilities waned compared to the boys, It became difficult to play with them anymore. Since I wasn't willing to give up on activities that relaxed me and gave me so much pleasure, I tried to convince my female friends to play with me. Not entiredly successful with my persuasion, I returned to the field to play with the boys. Certainly, puberty was a difficult stage, with several physical and social adjustments.

In school, I was loved by most of the teachers. I was a very good student; my grades were outstanding; but I wasn't sociable. I didn't care about interpersonal relationships. I spent most of my time participating in sports, my studies, my family, and playing alone. I was happiest creating my own worlds. To me, the world outside of me didn't measure up to my own inner reality.

I believed that sincerity was an essential pillar of interpersonal relationships. It was a quality that was very hard to find in other people. Lying and hypocrisy were predominant and, for some reason, my body rejected those characteristics with contempt. I didn't know where those feelings came from, or if they were good or bad. The solution then, was to escape to my inner world and stay in it until I felt safe enough to go to the outside world again.

All these things, in addition to the thousands of paranormal experiences that were had in the house, made me feel different from others. Most of these events happened to my older siblings; my younger brother and I didn't experience as many phenomena as them, but we lived in fear because of all the stories and events that they lived and felt. Among the paranormal experiences that they had, some more intense than others, were apparitions, out-of-body experiences, and abnormal resistance to waking up. I liked the idea of being different, but I didn't know at what point in my life this could be a disadvantage or make my life more complicated than normal. We never sought professional assistance. Basically, every once in a while, my mother brought the priest to bless the house. But I didn't notice too many changes after these sporadic blessings. I sensed that not all the entities were negative and disturbing. We were also surrounded by good spirits that protected us from negative aspects of the physical world.

The creepiest thing happened to my sister. She was lying in bed taking her afternoon nap and, when she woke up, she saw a short man walking around in her room. Since her eyes were still sleepy, she adjusted them to be sure of what she was seeing. Up until that point, the small man hadn't noticed that she was watching him. Once her sight was clear, she asked him with fearful voice, "Who are you? What are you doing here?"

The man turned around and stared at her without saying a single word. My sister wasn't sure if it was an entity or a physical presence. She could see every detail, but realized that the image of the man was blurry, which made her think that it was more likely an entity. Then she gathered her courage and asked him again, this time with a more emphatic tone of voice, "What are you looking for here?"

The man got upset and started beating everything around the room. His hands moved out of control from one side to the other. My sister got scared, cowered at the head of her bed, grabbed her pillow, and covered her eyes with it.

When the noise of ornaments falling to the floor stopped, my sister uncovered her face and looked around the room. The man was gone. It took all her strength to jump out of her bed and turn the light on. Her legs weren't working properly; she couldn't stand straight. She stretched out her hand to reach the doorknob, opened the door, and began to crawl to the next room, where my younger brother and I were watching TV. She entered the room with a pale face and terror in her eyes. As soon as we saw her, we knew something strange had happened to her, so we waited until she regained composure and told us. Then, my brother and I went to her room and saw the whole mess. Her stuff was strewn all across the floor, so we began to pick up each little ornament and put everything back in place.

Another chilling event was experienced by my older brother. Just like the rest of my siblings and me, he always waited for our nanny to enter his room with her songs to wake him up. That morning, he woke up on his own, but remained in bed with his eyes closed. Since Tata hadn't entered the room, he knew it was still early, and not yet time to get out of bed to get ready for school. The room was completely dark; my brother liked to sleep in complete darkness. In that state between asleep and awake, he felt that someone was sitting at the foot of his bed. He thought it was Tata, and was surprised that she wasn't singing any song. At that moment, he felt his blanket being taken away from him and began to feel the cold of the air conditioner on his feet. A bit upset by the unpleasant sensation, he spoke out in a disgruntled tone, "What are you doing? You're taking the blanket and I'm getting cold!"

Then, he felt two hands grab his ankles and, with impressive strength, he was pulled to the middle of his bed. With his heart racing, he opened his eyes and quickly stood up. He looked around but didn't see anybody. He rubbed the sleep from his eyes and looked again. Nothing. There was nobody around. He leaned toward the foot of his bed and looked down with fear. Once again, there was nothing. Not a single physical soul in the whole room except him. A few seconds later, Tata entered, turned the light on and saw him all stressed and scared.

"Sonny, what's wrong?"

Fearfully crying, my brother told her everything. Together, they kneeled to say a Lord's Prayer and offer three Hail Marys.

My brother talked about what had happened for weeks. All our friends and relatives found out and, once again, my mother brought a priest to cleanse the house with incense. The causes and consequences of all these things remain a mystery for everybody.

CHAPTER 2

Grief And Understanding

THE YEARS PASSED. My siblings and I grew up and graduated and the strange things kept happening in the house. But, by and large, they didn't affect us the same way anymore; we were used to them. Everything happened calmly in our lives, without highs or lows.

Until, one sad November night, my grandmother passed away. She was a sweet, loving, humanitarian, and a very spiritual woman. Her ancestors had been in contact with spirits for years, and many of them predicted big events that would take place in any part of the world. They even knew when and where they were going to die. Many of them asked to be taken to their native towns to die when they knew their time was near.

Strange occurences surrounded my grandmother's death. She had suffered a lung condition for years. The first time she relapsed, required her to be hospitalized in the intensive care unit. Once there, she had other health complications; her body was deteriorating. My aunt Belinda, who was a doctor, was also very spiritual. She had a mixed character of strong and soft, with oriental-looking brown eyes, a round face, dark hair, and a huge devotion to helping with the healing of others. But she didn't give us false hope. My Grandma's condition was getting worse as the days passed.

During this time of uncertainty, my grandmother shared several of her experiences with us. She told us that she had seen her mother, or rather she had been introduced to her. My grandmother hadn't known her mother, who had died giving birth to my grandmother. My grandmother was the only connection I had left to my great-grandmother Rosa. There weren't any pictures or letters … no memories at all. Her mother was a name without a face. My grandmother's aunts and other relatives, who had already gone to the spiritual world, offered the introduction. Grandma was very happy to finally meet her mother and see several of her relatives again. She told us that there had been a meeting to decide if she would stay with us or if she would go to the other side.

Two days later, Grandma wanted to talk to my Aunt Belinda alone. She explained that the decision to stay or go was up to her, but that she also had been allowed to see part of what her future would be. Because of what she saw, she decided to leave for the other side. Everything would be fast; it was just a matter of days.

"You have to let me go," my Grandma said to Aunt Belinda.

With tears in her eyes, my aunt answered, "Mommy, I don't want to see you suffer. I believe in you and your decisions. Do whatever God asks you to do, even if it's going to be a big loss for me. I'll respect your decision and the Lord's." My grandmother was very glad to hear my aunt's words so she could leave in peace.

Before passing away, Grandma shared with us. "There will be many unions and separations. More people will arrive to be part of the family; many will join me on the other side. Be ready; always bear in mind that, to live with dignity, to be in service to the Lord, we must love, be kind, be humanitarian, be humble, and compassionate. We must pursue the peace within each one of us, so we can carry it and pass it on to others to make this world a better place."

The next day, Grandma told us that some people she didn't know tried to take her, but she told them to go away, that she would never go with them. Grandma let us know that the experience had been pretty unpleasant, that she felt fear and anguish, but luckily, they left her alone.

That was my grandmother's last night in this world. Her passing deeply marked our whole family, even though we had all witnessed her reassuring words, experiences, and advice. It was hard for many of my family members to go on without her.

That sad night, a dark night without moon and stars, and with my grief-stricken heart, I wrote a poem for my beloved grandmother when I got home:

"Blessing, God bless you"
My granny tells me from heaven
I stare at her star
I believe that I talk to her
Suddenly, I hear her voice
"You only have to look
Inside your heart
You will discover
That I am there
When you cry, I will cry
If you need me, I will be there
When you want to talk
I will always be able to listen
I will come at night

To make you sleep in my arms
And then I will tell you
How much I love you."

I showed the poem to my mother. Her tear-filled eyes implored me. I became so concerned about my mother that I stopped thinking about my grandmother. I decided to focus on taking care of my mother and other relatives who had suffered the passing of my grandmother without any consolation.

The night of the wake, a man I didn't know sat next to me. I only knew that he was a relative of one of my aunts-in-law. His smile and his company made me feel at peace. Then, he spoke to me. "Hi. My name is Amasis. You're Rosa's daughter, aren't you? The youngest of the women?"

"Yes, and you? Are you a relative of my Aunt Constantina?"

"Yes, I'm her brother. Here, where I am, I can see very interesting things, and I hear very interesting things as well."

"Like what?"

"Well, I can see your grandfather enjoying the company of your grandmother at home in the wonderful world.

"My grandfather died of Leukemia about twenty-seven years ago."

"Well, in what people know as the spiritual world," Amasis said, "I see several of your grandmother's relatives who have already passed away, welcoming and guiding her. She is very happy. Obviously, she doesn't suffer any physical pain and enjoys the peace and harmony of the spiritual world. Now, the grief of her daughters and sons and other relatives who still remain on this eartly side, afflicts and saddens her a bit. It will just be a matter of time until she is able to fully enjoy her stay at home. In time, you'll stop crying and suffering in your souls and thus she'll be able to get free from all the ties of anguish that she still senses.

Completely amazed, I tried to process all the things that this man was telling me in my mind. After a while, I was curious about what he was listening to.

"What things have you heard that you find so interesting?"

He smiled, turned to face me completely and told me, "I was expecting that question kiddo, so they are right in what they say. Well, child, they tell me that you are one of our kind, that the Holy Spirit has granted you gifts, and that you have certain missions in this life. I sat next to you to prove what they told me and I just realized that it is so. I read the poem that you wrote for your grandmother. It made me think that there was something different in you and now I know what it is. Don't worry or be scared by the way this works. Little by little, the divine doors will be opening. You'll be receiving the messages at the right time and place and you will help some people directly and others indirectly. Now, to carry out all the tasks and missions, you'll have to make contact with the spiritual world. This will also happen slowly. You'll be given a spiritual guide in the spiritual world and an earthly guide in this earthly world. Several times, your pride will be tested, and you will want to give up. You will lose that desire to help, but your earthly guide will give you the necessary explanations for you to go on. The first thing you need to know and embrace is that God is omniscient. He can see and do everything and his will is a priority above all."

For some reason, I understood a lot of what Mr. Amasis said to me.

"You are one of our own. I can see the influence of the angels in your poetry. You'll bring messages to your loved ones to guide them on their pathways. Your earthly guidance will be given to you very soon."

"Will you be my earthly guide?" I asked him

"Most likely, yes."

My mother called me from afar. She needed me to go to the car and get one of the thank-you notes for one of her friends, who was about to leave. Just like my mother asked me, I went to the car, got the card, gave it to her, and said goodbye to her friend. I went to look for Mr. Amasis, but he wasn't sitting on the bench anymore. I looked all around the place, but I couldn't find him.

When I got home, I told my mother about my conversation with Amasis. After all, she knew more about him than I did and I wanted to know what she thought about what he'd said. She told me about all the times when Amasis had served as a medium in the communication between our dead relatives and us. According to my mother, he was a very spiritually-elevated man. When he had approached me, I'd had my own impressions. They had been 100 percent positive. Everything my mother told me had a powerful impact on me and confirmed what I already felt. I became interested in knowing how Amasis and my ancestors had managed to obtain that level of spiritual enlightenment and knowledge.

My mother got out of her bed when she realized my concerns and desire to go further with all of this. She opened her wardrobe, took a book out and placed it in my hands. The book was about how the spiritual movement had started in our family from former times. The book had been written by a regional author who was a distant relative of ours. Very excited, I read the book from the beginning to the end before the day was over.

The story tells about a French man by the pen name of Allan Kardec who wrote two books: *The Spirits' Book* and *The Book on Mediums*. These books were in the hands of the Carmonas, a Spanish family. They were given to them so they could spread the information in Latin America. The Carmonas owned a circus. When the circus came to Venezuela, it passed by the town where my family used to live. This town was mostly populated by people of independent thinking and without religious prejudices, which made it an ideal situation for adopting and spreading Spiritualist doctrines. The ideas of the people were progressive and rationalist. My relatives were quite interested in studying and elaborating on the philosophical and ethical doctrines that had invaded Europe, mainly France, England, Spain, and Italy. The Spiritualist Center was founded by my ancestors in April of 1882.

Allan Kardec explained that the Spiritism doctrine consoled and explained several of the psychological and spiritual problems that haunted mankind. The book dealt with several interesting subjects such as: telepathy, clairvoyance, precognition, child prodigies of art and math, reincarnation, the mind, the unconscious mind, the transmuter and the transmuted, time machines, all kinds of experiences through hypnosis, the control of the mind, the telekinesis specialists, diagnosis of diseases through the dreams, and publications by different local authors about Spiritism, parapsychology, and related sciences.

Fascinated with what I was reading, I ran to my mother and nanny to tell them and exchange opinions about the different subjects. My mother, seeing that much interest in me about a particular subject, and my knowing my ability to analyze and give meaning to many of the subjects described, ventured to tell me some stories about our Spiritualist relatives.

Her Aunt Rebecca was the one who experienced paranormal events. My mother told me two stories about her Aunt Rebecca that marked her forever.

"Aunt Rebecca was combing her hair to go to bed after dinner around six thirty on the hot night of February 5, 1980. Suddenly, a shocking 'Oooww!' was heard, and then a thick, trembling voice, unlike Aunt Rebecca's, came out of her mouth. A spirit had possessed her and spoke, 'I'm a spirit in the dark because the temptation of the flesh maddened me with jealousy to the point of taking the life of a handsome young man who was just beginning to taste the sweetness of clandestine love. The rage of having shared the fresh apple that I believed to be my exclusive property drove me to shoot the young man in the back.

"'They've allowed me to join to this subject in order to witness before the Heavenly Father and before you, my brothers, to my sincere repentance, for which I kneel and beg for your forgiveness, and thus, once cleansed from sin, ask the Lord to give me the light to bless a couple whose son has my blood running through his veins, so they have the divine protection of the Almighty in this earthly transitory stage, where evil turns into good in the generation that they belong to. I leave confident in forgiveness.'

"Aunt Rebecca returned to normality, asked for some brandy and totally calmed and fell asleep."

To me, the story was interesting and frightening at the same time. The fact that a spirit had taken over her body sounded unpleasant to me. Getting more excited, my mother wanted to tell me the other story of my aunt right away. She said I was going to like it even more because it was in a historical context.

"On November 22, 1963, around one o'clock, Aunt Rebecca, already blind and elderly, got out of bed, raised her hands to touch her silver hair and exclaimed, 'My God! I've seen a man collapse. He seemed an important politician riding in a convertible in the middle of a big gathering of people, and accompanied by an elegant woman. But he didn't die a natural death. He was despicably murdered by a man in the crowd.'

"My aunt paused and then continued. 'Yes! That man died and I see them taking him away to be buried. But it's strange,… they don't carry him in a modern hearse, but in a cart driven by beautiful horses. He must be a very important person because the funeral procession extends along a large avenue, and there are floral offerings and guards of honor as well.'

"My aunt went back to normal and looked tired and sweaty. One hour and a half after my aunt had had this experience, we heard on TV the announcement of the murder of President John F. Kennedy in the city of Dallas, Texas. According to the records, Kennedy was shot at 12:30 PM, Dallas time. That was 2:30 PM in Caracas, one hour and a half after Aunt Rebecca's premonition."

These stories made me think that we had to continue along this pathway. Maybe Grandma's passing would be the opportunity to resume everything.

CHAPTER 3

The Messages Begin

SIX MONTHS WENT BY since Grandma's passing and things gradually went back to normal. The family still met for weddings, birthdays, anniversaries, graduations, and other special events but the mood wasn't the same. Many of my relatives began to deal with unpleasant situations in their lives at an economic, physical, and family level. There were illnesses and separations. For some time, I didn't feel well knowing that many of my relatives were suffering, and I wasn't there to support them because I was always busy with work. I had to travel a lot both within and outside the country. I always found out about some bad news on the phone when I was away, and my heart and soul complained about that.

I felt that life was about studying, graduating, working, and climbing the ladder in order to haved a good quality of life for me and my loved ones. But I didn't know if I was doing all the things that would ensure my happiness. One depressing night, I prayed to the Lord, and I asked him to, somehow, grant me a tool that would allow me to be a guide or a comfort for all my loved ones in their times of suffering, and let me be a cure in their moments of sickness, and a hand and a hug in happiness. I fell deeply asleep after I finished praying and when I woke up I felt that, after several weeks, I had finally had a good, refreshing rest.

I called home and found out everything was fine. That day, I'd be flying back home. I was very happy and feeling a lot of energy. When I got to the airport, I found out the flight was delayed due to a problem with the airplane. I didn't know or care about the details, but they told us that it would take only thirty minutes to resolve. I went to get something to eat because waiting and uncertainty always stimulated my appetite.

Returning to the departure gate, I was told that the problem with the airplane would take much longer so we would be boarding another airplane. It would take off in three hours. I was willing to wait, as long as could to get home that same evening, so I started walking around the airport. It was very small. I walked through the entire place in about fifteen minutes. So I bought a magazine. The cover looked interesting, but the content was poor. I still wasn't a very sociable person, so interacting with other passengers wasn't an option for me. I decided to get ahead on some work. I turned my laptop on and plugged it into a power outlet. When I checked my files, I noticed that I didn't have any pending work; everything was done.

My cell phone rang. It was my mother, who wanted to know if everything was okay, and if she still had to pick me at the airport at the agreed upon time. I should have called her, but I had forgotten since I was usually picked up by a driver from the company. I told her about all the delays and told her to expect my phone call when I was able to board the airplane. She told me that everything was fine there. Only my Aunt Belinda was a bit concerned and distressed with the economic situation she was going through. We would have to talk about that later.

I hung up the phone, took out the laptop and put it on my lap. All of a sudden, I started writing spontaneously. *Your crying doesn't stop me from being where I have to be. It's all a matter of time. Hard days will come, but let yourself be guided by your instincts; I will give you signals. You were a very good daughter. I love you and I always will forever.*

I stopped writing just as quickly as I had started. I felt the words were coming from my grandmother and that it was a message for my aunt. Without thinking, I sent it in an e-mail to my aunt and told her that it was a message from my grandmother.

My aunt came with my mother to pick me at the airport. She didn't want to wait another second to ask me about what had happened. I answered, "Auntie, it really wasn't anything supernatural. I just turned my computer on and started writing the message …"

My aunt responded, "Julia, you don't know how happy this makes me. I've been crying over Mom all this time. I've always known that crying doesn't help them to go up to heaven. That's why, even when I couldn't control my crying, I felt terrible for not letting her go up and go with God … but Mom has relieved me with her words. The other things she told you in this message are premonitions; she shows me that in the future I'll find challenges and bad times, but she advises me to stand it, and she will give me the signals to overcome them. Thanks, Chichita."

I smiled in return at her affectionate use of my nickname.

God had heard me. Even when I was away working, I was able to be useful in helping my family recover from their grief. Indeed, my aunt and her family went through very hard times. She did just as grandma had told her; she followed her instincts and was always expectant for more signals.

I woke up very early one Saturday morning. I drank some coffee, read the news, and fanned my face with the newspaper. There was an intense heat. The smell of coffee would always awaken my muses and, apparently, my connection with the other world. Suddenly, I felt like typing.

My daughter, now, more than ever, you have to trust yourself. Don't listen to anybody; just let yourself be guided by your instincts. Don't look for explanations to the things that don't have any explanation in the earthly world. You have to act alone. Otherwise, you'll regret it for the rest of your life. I'll take care of you in the hard times. I love you, my daughter. Goodbye.

I ran to the telephone and called my aunt to give her the message. Even though I didn't express my happiness, I marveled internally for being able to be in touch with my grandmother, and for being an instrument to help my aunt to overcome the hard times she was going through.

Things slowly got better in the family at a general level. All of my grandmother's premonitions came true and both good and bad were accepted and handled with faith and obedience, respecting the Lord's will above all.

Two years after my grandmother's passing, and after helping my family to connect with the other world and to overcome hard situations, I got a proposal from my boss. There was a job opening in a city in Canada. My experience and skill could be utilized for the success of the company and the advancement would be key for my career development.

I sat down with my mother and my nanny to evaluate the proposal. The benefits, salary, and my professional development looked much better than my current situation. My mother advised me to take the chance and request that, at least once a year, the company would pay my round-trip tickets to come home and visit at Christmas. I did it. I told my boss that I was willing to accept the challenge, but only on the condition that I could see my family once a year. My boss accepted immediately.

The farewell was a bit sad but, with the approval of my mother and my nanny, I boarded the airplane to my northern adventure without looking back. I felt good about ensuring a better future for me and all my loved ones.

CHAPTER 4

The Encounter I

S ETTLING IN TO A new country, a new job, a new way of life, wasn't easy at first. I missed my home and my family. But, I liked my new job. Most of the days in the city were sunny, depending on the season. In summer, the sun rose pretty early, around 5 AM, and in winter, it came up around 8 AM. The road I took to work was quite pleasant. The river I passed by was always so mysterious and energetic in the mornings, with its brown tones and a strong and impressive current.

The traffic was often really slow, depending on the time of day that you commuted and what streets you took. Regardless of the traffic in the center of the city, the harmony of colors, sounds, and smells of the natural world that surrounded it, framed the core with a relaxing and pleasant environment.

Tall buildings sprang from the downtown core: pleasant and elegant architecture with massive glass windows and supported by the latest technology.

Early in the morning, hundreds of people ate their breakfast in the food courts of their workplaces. These people were in groups, talking, reading the newspaper, enjoying their food and the company of friends and coworkers.

Men wore elegant suits and shirts in pastel colors such as lilac and pink. They looked very elegant with polished shoes and neatly combed hair. Women, also elegant, were immaculately dressed and wore natural-looking make-up.

The lines in the coffee shops were exaggeratedly long, and the amounts of coffee that the people bought and drank during the day were exorbitant.

At work, between e-mails and meetings, the time flew for me. At lunchtime, I used to go to eat in my favorite places around 12 PM, but eventually, I realized that noon was the worst time to go. All the places were completely full and the service wasn't very good. Thus, I found out that the best time to eat was half an hour before noon or one hour after noon. Walking through the park at noon was a better choice. These walks through the park were the best moments of the day, and I enjoyed them significantly.

In the park, I could breathe in a lot of peace and tranquility; I could feel the grass cradling me, the skies wrapping around me, and the winds numbing me. The sounds were diverse and inspiring just like in the summer: ducks quacking, the birds lulling chirps, the river current, and the whisper of the tree leaves.

In autumn, some days were gray. But different combinations of colors, red and violet tones with brown and yellow remained in the flowers. Falling leaves would blow in the wind, while the trees swayed as if they were giving a warm greeting. The crunchy, fallen leaves created an artistic path on the grass. Sometimes, the wind would blow so softly you could barely feel it, and other times, so strong that it could lift you from the ground. The place was impregnated with the smell of pine trees. The river was calmer at this hour, with a gorgeous turquoise color reflected from the clear sky above.

During this time of the year, you still could see people walking, jogging, and doing all kinds of exercises in the park. Many would take their dogs out for a walk, and you could also see fathers or groups of mothers entertaining their children.

There was a bridge leading to another park. That park was everyone's favorite place to do exercises because there was a staircase with 162 steps. I climbed them several times, but I always ran out of breath before I reached the top, and I had to stop to rest several times along the way. Without exaggerating, the sensation of reaching the top was heart stopping. Still, the view from the top was spectacular, and worth the effort. I could see the river and the buildings at the center of the city; it made me feel like my soul had returned to my body.

Everything was perfect; I discovered myself effortlessly and without pain. I was able to connect with myself and produce only love while receiving the blessings of the greater universe. I was beginning to feel at home in my new country. I invited my mind to rest, and my body and soul to perceive, to fill each one of the holes inside of me.

Two months passed. I had finally found an apartment with all the comforts that I was looking for. Once everything was under control, I decided to look for a gym. The exercises and sports relaxed me and helped clear my mind, besides keeping me in shape. Over the last few years, I had dedicated myself to work too much, and I had neglected my health. Canada was known for providing excellent services in areas such as health and well-being.

I had been looking for a couple weeks when I finally found a club. It was better than just a gym because, at this club, I could do exercises and practice my sports in the same place. It was pretty convenient from a time and fuel-saving point of view. It also had a restaurant which, from the social side of things, would make it easier for me to meet people and make friends. Once I signed up and paid for my membership, they offered me the services of a personal trainer. I wasn't so sure if that was a good idea or not. I had been doing exercises on my own and had read several books about exercising, so I felt confident in being able to do exercises by myself. Anyway, I accepted a first appointment with the trainer since it was free.

The week went by really quickly. I was very busy with work and for a moment I thought about canceling my appointment. I was too tired, and I didn't want to feel tied to anything. I just wanted to go to the gym when I felt like, doing my exercises and going back home. Just when I decided to cancel my appointment, the trainer called me to remind me about it. Her voice was energetic and enthusiastic, totally opposed to my mood; somehow, she managed to pass her enthusiasm to me and convinced me to meet later.

While I was going home, I began to think of excuses for not going to the appointment. The traffic was heavy, and I felt tired and in a bad mood. But, I argued with myself, I was closer to the gym than home.

I went to the desk and asked for Khrystal. They called her on the speakers, and she came down the stairs in a few seconds with a smile on her face.

"Hi. Julia, isn't it?" she asked as she extended her hand toward me.

"Yes, and you ... you're Khrystal?"

She smiled and nodded.

Right away, she started to explain everything to me: all the tests that she was going to make me do, one by one, and their goals. She talked too fast. Although my English was good there were some words that I didn't recognize sometimes, so I had to ask her to talk slower. I explained that I hadn't been in Canada long.

"Where are you from?" she asked.

"Venezuela."

"Yes,… and what brought you here? I'm not familiar with Venezuela or any other South American country yet, but I've heard several times that Venezuela and most of the South American countries are spectacular because of their nature, people, food, and traditions."

"Yes, the landscapes and places are beautiful. Although in these last years, we haven't been doing too well in political, economic, and social terms. I got a transfer through the company that I work for, and I'm very happy to be here now. They needed someone with my experience, and I wanted to look around and assess the quality of life." I paused, looked directly into her eyes and resumed. "I might stay longer than I thought. Maybe this is my home. In my country, it was very hard for me to interact with people. I hope that it will change and that I find a better understanding and way of life with the people here."

"I always heard the people in your country are very friendly, kind, generous, warm, and very familiar," Khrystal commented.

"Yes, that's all true. I've been here for just two months and I really miss my people and my traditions. It's just that, at a professional level, I can't find compatibility. I hope it will be different here. So far, it has been! I've felt good about my job and my coworkers. There are several projects, many things to be done and improved."

The conversation stopped there so I could begin taking the tests. Once I was finished, Khrystal printed the report, sat down, read it carefully and then explained it to me. To improve my health and wellbeing, I had to make some changes. She showed me a plan called *periodization*, where my exercise program was divided into several stages. Each stage had a purpose, and eventually, putting it all together, I would lose some weight and gain muscle mass.

I got home really tired that day. I fell on my bed like a rock. Then, I got out of bed at midnight because I was very thirsty. I went to the kitchen and had a glass of water. While drinking the water, I saw a light coming through the window. It was the full moon, brighter than ever. I stared at it for about fifteen minutes before going back to bed.

Early in the morning, I remembered my dream: I was in some sort of carriage, and the sound of the wheels touching the ground repeated over and over in my head. I also dreamed about a small girl, maybe five years old, standing behind a wooden fence. I could barely see her but I knew she was staring at me. It seemed to me, that things were starting to get a bit strange, just like in my childhood and teen years.

My job stopped being motivating for a while. The projects were delayed, and the tasks became pretty routine, not requiring my creativity and analytical sense, so I decided that it was the right time to deal with my personal matters.

Training with Khrystal was really fun, and I started seeing the results of our sessions. I was very happy with myself and the way I looked. Clothes weren't a problem anymore. I went to the stores, picked some clothes in my size without trying them on, and when I got home and put them on, they would actually fit.

I felt a lot of energy, and I did much better with housekeeping and work. The confidence that I felt from looking good and being happy with my job was reflected in my interpersonal relationships, which improved significantly. I couldn't believe what I saw inside of me. I felt happier, laughed more than ever, everything was bright. I always had positive words and saw life in a new light. Khrystal and I got along great; she really helped me to settle in the city, always giving me advice about where to go, what to buy, about the culture and people in general.

Since I was her last client of the day, we stayed to talk about any subject for hours after our sessions. She seemed pretty interested in knowing about my culture, food, music, and interesting places. One afternoon, a workmate invited me to have some drinks, but I couldn't accept because I had an appointment with Khrystal, so I told her that we could go any other day. She asked me why, and I thought it was odd because the people around here don't usually ask personal questions. Nobody, just nobody, meddles in the affairs of others. Even though I thought it was strange, I told her where I was going and told her a bit about Khrystal and how well we got along. I also told her that Khrystal had group classes. My workmate didn't show any interest, and then warned me that I shouldn't think that my relationship with Khrystal was sincere.

"Julia, don't believe she's your friend or something like that. She only wants to make a living off your payments …" my friend warned me.

"I've got the results that I was looking for. I'm not thinking about renewing. She's taught me many things, and I believe that I can go on by myself, but I owe her everything I've achieved so far."

"You owe everything to her? Well, in part. The discipline of going to the gym, the will to do everything she makes you do, and the ability to pay for her services … that's all yours. Don't be confused. The people around here are not like the people in your land. Here, you're just a monetary value to someone, and it's all alright until you're not it anymore. Then you'll see the other side of the coin, dear."

Her words got me worried. I really liked Khrystal and, more than a trainer, she was a friend to me. My workmate was from this area and she knew more about the people and the culture than I did. Everything was fine so far, so I decided to give it time to see what happened.

When I got to the gym, Khrystal was waiting for me with a nice warm smile. That day, I was really exhausted after the training and I noticed that Khrystal was in low spirits, perhaps tired after a long day of work.

"Khrystal, is everything alright?" I asked.

"Yes and no."

"What is it?"

"Well, today I broke up with my boyfriend. He'd been my boyfriend since I was thirteen years old. We had almost everything arranged to get married, but something tells me he's not the man of my life."

"After all the time you've been together, and after all the arrangements, how can you think that he's not the man you want to spend the rest of your life with?" I asked.

"Well, I felt doubt when I met someone a few months ago. I felt things that I'd never felt before, and even though nothing has happened between us, I feel different when I'm with him, which made me think that I was just with my ex-boyfriend out of habit."

"Are you sure, Khrystal? Now, does this other guy feel the same about you?"

"He has a girlfriend right now. I don't know his feelings for me, but I believe that he does feel something. I don't care right now anyway, I need to stay away from my ex-boyfriend to experience things without him and truly realize if I love him or if it's just that I'm used to him."

"Does he know that you're suggesting some time apart, or does he believe it's over?"

"He thinks it's over."

"What if you realize that it's love, and when you want to get back together, he's no longer there for you? What if somebody else comes into his life?"

"That would prove that he's not the one for me. That way, he could find his real pathway, and I would have to start walking mine."

I didn't say anything else to Khrystal, but to me it was obvious that she didn't feel anything for her ex-boyfriend at that moment.

That night, I had those strange dreams again. The ride on the carriage repeated itself over and over. This time, I could see a man who seemed to be my father, a girl to my right and a boy to my left. Apparently, they were my sister and brother, and I was sitting on my mother's lap. She was a dark-haired woman with black eyes, white skin, and very elegantly dressed. Once again, in the distance, I saw the five-year-old girl behind the fence. This time, I could get a better look at her eyes; they were blue, innocent, but sad.

I woke up wanting to know more. I wondered what those dreams were about. I called my mother and asked her to give me the phone numbers of Amasis. My mom had to call my aunt. Then she called me back and gave them to me. Without thinking too much about it, I called him. Unfortunately, I couldn't connect with him. But I left my number and a message asking him to call me back as soon as possible.

It was almost time for my next appointment with Khrystal – to take some tests and measure my progress. When I arrived at the gym, I couldn't find a spot in the parking lot because it was a busy time of day. I asked the young receptionist where I could park because I had an appointment now, but I couldn't find a place to park for almost twenty minutes. The young girl told me that in these cases, they would always set up the parking lot in the back, so I could park there and go through the back door into the trainers' room.

When I entered the parking lot at the back, I noticed that there was a wooden fence just like the one I'd seen in my dreams. I thought that it was very strange that there was a wooden fence, like the ones that you see in the stables, here at a gym in the city. The fence was half-finished. It was as if that facility had been a house or a farm many years ago and it had been turned into a gym.

Upon entering the building, I met one of the club's owners. I asked him what the place had been before it was turned into a gym. He told me that it used to be a warehouse, but he didn't have any information about what it was before that. I started having strange ideas. The gym could have been my home in the times of my dreams. Maybe that place wasn't new to me at all. Khrystal came out to greet me, smiling as usual.

After she had gone over all the results of the evaluations with me, I was very happy with them. Then she asked me if I wanted to renew more sessions and, since I had already thought about it, I didn't renew. I felt fine with myself; it was just a matter of maintaining all that I had achieved. Nevertheless, she asked me to think about it. I was very clear that I didn't want to purchase any more sessions. I said goodbye and left to watch a hockey game.

I was at home, reading a Paulo Coelho book before going to bed, when I started seeing rain falling right in front of me. I heard thunder, in the dark. To my complete surprise, I saw a woman who looked exactly like Khrystal. I saw all of this through a blurry window floating in the air. It was like a projection of my mind, but then I saw the man that I've been dreaming about, who was my father, enter the scene. They were in some sort of kitchen from the 1800s. She was talking to him, begging him. My father was making gestures as if he was upset … it seemed as if he was trying to end his relationship with her. She held his hands and put them on her breasts, then sat on the kitchen table and started kissing him passionately. My father took her in his arms, lifted her skirt and started making love to her. I looked to one side and then to the other, and there wasn't anybody around.

Suddenly, everything disappeared, and I was back in my house, with the book in my hands. "Who are these people and what were these visions about?" I wondered aloud.

As the days went by, just like my coworker had warned me, Khrystal changed her behavior and disposition with me from the moment I wasn't her client anymore. I felt bad. I really was fond of her. Her company had been pleasant, and she had really helped me to settle into the city. On several occasions, I tried to meet with her. She always told me that she was busy and could not talk to me. I realized that her workplace was not the best for socializing. So I suggested that we go out together to have coffee or dinner, but she always had an appointment or some plans with someone else.

Other trainers, who also liked me, approached me to tell me that Khrystal didn't speak too well about me, so it was better for me to turn away. All of this was very strange. I hadn't done anything to her, I was just trying to be friendly. At the same time, I wondered if, without realizing and without any wrong intent, I had offended her somehow.

I decided to go shopping over the weekend. While I was looking at the showcases and buying accessories that I needed, I saw some very cute pink earrings. I fell in love with them, so I entered the store and asked their price. Since they were at a very good price, I suddenly thought that I could give them to Khrystal. It had been her birthday two weeks before. I had remembered about her birthday and congratulated her, but I didn't have a present for her that day because I hadn't found anything that I liked. I bought the earrings, wrapped them in paper, and took them to the gym.

"When do you have a break?" I asked her.

"Right now I have a client, and two more after her, and then my boyfriend comes to pick me up to go out with some friends."

"Okay, so you're back with your boyfriend?"

"Oh, I thought I had told you."

"No, we haven't really talked since the day you evaluated me."

"Yes, that's true. It's just that I've been too busy but, well, I have to go … but yes, I'm back with my boyfriend."

That moment, the receptionist came to tell her that her client had called to cancel her appointment because she wasn't feeling well. Khrystal looked at me and said, "Well then, I have fifteen minutes. I have to start working on my next clients' programs after that."

"Okay, I don't think I'll need more than fifteen minutes."

"Okay, good."

"Khrystal, how do you feel now that you're back with your boyfriend?"

"Honestly, not too different. I think I've definitely realized that I don't feel anything for him anymore."

"And what happened with the other young man?"

"He broke up with his girlfriend and he's just like me, totally sure that she's not what he wants."

"And then …?"

"Well, he doesn't love her, but he also doesn't want to be involved in a serious relationship. He wants to have a good time, enjoy, travel, and experience the world.

"And what do you think about that?"

"I'm looking for exactly the same things he's looking for: a relationship that doesn't represent an attachment or a formality. Maybe just traveling the world, enjoying it, having fun."

"Does that mean that you could be a couple, but with no ties or responsibilities?"

"Yes, exactly."

"Do you think that might work?

"I hope so because my feelings for him are sincere. I just understand that his last relationship was somewhat traumatic and he doesn't want to get involved right now. Besides, things are more complicated because he also works here. He's one of the trainers."

"Really? Which one is him?"

"His name is Bob, that one over there, standing next to the man with black sweatpants."

I turned around to see him; he was a trainer that I had already seen other times, always with a stuck-up attitude, and making every single young woman near him fall for him.

"Oh, okay. Yes, I've seen him before. By the way, before you leave, I want to give you a birthday present."

She smiled. I took the earrings out of my purse and gave them to her. She unwrapped the box and opened it, anxious to see what was inside. Once she saw the earrings, her face completely changed. She closed the box and gave it back to me.

"I can't accept such an expensive gift. The gym doesn't allow me to accept things like these, or having close relationships with members that used to be my clients."

"Okay, but I bought them for you. I don't want them. What do I do with them?"

"I don't know. That's your problem, not mine."

I couldn't believe what was going on. In my whole life, I had never dealt with something like that. I turned around with the earrings in my hand and left the gym right away. On my way out, I noticed the wooden fence again, and I wondered *What's wrong with me? What were all these dreams and visions about?* Then, I remembered that the woman in my vision looked exactly like Khrystal, and I also wondered, *Why Khrystal?*

Once back home, I heard the voices of children coming and going all over the place. I asked myself, *What is this? What kind of message are they trying to pass across with these visions.*

CHAPTER 5

Closure

Abstract a year passed by and I was still going to the same gym. I met and traveled around several small towns near the city where I lived. My whole family visited me, and we walked around and went to the best places, hotels, and restaurants. We had great times, and I thanked God from the bottom of my heart for every moment, for every chance.

When I went to the gym, Khrystal was always there, but we didn't talk or treat each other like we used to do. Every three months, new employees were hired, and others quit to pursue other opportunities. I really got along with Jenn, one of the new trainers. She was very spiritual, happy, and she transmitted her good vibes. I felt comfortable with her and started telling her about all the strange things that I had been dreaming, seeing, and living this last year. Jenn thought that all those experiences were spectacular.

The dreams continued, and the visions became clearer every day. One afternoon, I leaned back because I didn't feel well. I felt like I was about to catch a cold. I fell asleep for a while and I saw a letter in my mind. The paper had colored with age; I guessed that it was from long

ago. The writing was surprisingly legible for being so old, so I began
to read it:

Let me love you
And thus the roses shall bloom in the garden
Let me make you happy
And see your smile with every sunset
Let me be your shadow, your shelter,
And fill your eyes with hopes
Draw your dreams with brushes
Root out your sorrows
You are and forever will be my life
You are like water to life
You are a heavenly muse to a poet
You are life, motivation, hope and love
You are my oxygen; you are the essence of my existence
You are the reason why my heart never stops
The reason why my soul enjoys and dances a waltz of roses
And my voice sings the most beautiful love songs
You are the light that illuminates my thoughts
The engine of my greatest achievements
The hands that help me to build a better world
The mantle that I wrap my dreams with.

With lots of love,
John

I woke up right after I'd finished reading the letter. On the sofa in front
of my bed, I saw and image of my father from 1813. I had found this
number everywhere, so I assumed that it was the date where I was in
the memories of my past life. Without moving his lips, my father began

to communicate telepathically. He told me, "They have given me the chance to explain everything to you. I don't have too much time, but I need you to know that you have to prevent a calamity."

I still didn't understand anything.

My father talked to me again. "My name is John. Your name, and your mother's name in this life that we shared, was Sarah. I made the mistake of being unfaithful to your mother with a woman who wasn't of my class, but who fulfilled my fantasies. It wasn't love or passion, just fun. But she got pregnant by me, and a baby girl was born. I never loved her, never took care of her, and never wanted to know anything about her. This woman named Leslie, died giving birth to our daughter and her maternal grandmother Laurie took care of her. The night she was born, I sat in my office, having just found out she was born, and decided not to know anything else about them. I decided that you would be my only family, that I would never do something like that again, and that your mother was the light of my eyes and the only woman meant for me. I closed that chapter of my life and I thought I had ended everything. I took all of our properties, sold them, and we moved far from that place. But, I couldn't get rid of the spell that Laurie had put on me, with the deepest hate in her heart. She had lost the apple of her eye that night, her favorite and most beautiful daughter.

"I didn't live for too long after that. Two years later, I suffered an unknown illness that had no cure. The doctors didn't understand or know what to do for me and ever since then, I've been locked with Leslie in a dark place where evil prevails. I've asked the higher souls to commiserate with me and help me to prevent Khrystal's death. Since there was a time when you were my flesh and blood, I promised to pay my debts through you."

"But I don't get it," I commented. "Why Khrystal? Who is she in this story?"

"She's the reincarnation of my daughter. She's your half-sister."

For a moment, the communication was lost. My soul rejected the idea; everything became very complicated. We connected again after a while.

"I don't have much time, Julia," he repeated. "You always were the daughter that filled my heart with joy. You really were a role model and my pride. Please, help me ... Khrystal is deeply in love with a young man who doesn't feel the same for her. It takes a longer time for him to feel something for her. Even if he marries her in a few years, she will never be the world to him. She's considering getting pregnant to make him marry her. The responsibility of having a child is the last thing he wants at this moment in his life. He will force her out of his life, she will go on with the idea of having the baby, and will die just like Leslie, giving birth. I need you to go where she is and tell her not to do it, that she shouldn't seek to get pregnant."

My father sounded very disturbed and as if it was a state of emergency. I couldn't see or hear him anymore, but I did feel an external energy pushing me. I felt like I had all the right in the world to warn her. I took my car keys and, without thinking, I went to the gym at full speed.

When I arrived at the gym, I met my friend Jenn and asked her for Khrystal. She pointed to where Khrystal was training one of her clients. I approached her and pleaded, "Khrystal, I need to talk to you."

"I'm sorry, Julia, but right now I'm busy with her, and I have clients until the end of the day. I don't even have five minutes to rest."

"It's important," I insisted.

Khrystal noticed the urgency in my eyes. "Can you wait for me to finish with all my clients? And ... well, I have plans with Bob, so it'll have to be brief."

"Yes, it's pretty brief," I promised.

Jenn was watching and listening to everything from the back of the room. I went to sit at a table outside the small room. Jenn came to me and said, "Julia, I really don't know what kind of relationship you and Khrystal have. She makes derogatory comments about you. She feels like you're stalking her, that you have some sort of obsession for her, giving her things, and she doesn't know how to get rid of you."

I answered, "I have missions in this life and, unfortunately, she's one of the people that I have to help spiritually, Jenn. I know that not everybody can understand this, and I know it sounds crazy, but it's true. Now I have something extremely important to tell her."

"I just want to stop her from hurting you, and I want the gossip around the gym every day to be over as well," Jenn stressed.

"I really value and appreciate what you do, Jenn. You're a really nice person and I acknowledge your intentions. Let me tell you, I know Khrystal is a hypocrite. She says nasty things behind my back, but she flatters me when we are alone. But I don't care about that, I have to do what I came here for."

"Julia, you should stop your spiritual missions! Khrystal only humiliates you, and you let her do it because of the esteem that you have for her."

"I can't change the world or what the world thinks of me. I can only do what I think is right. To you, I'm being humiliated."

"Yes, Julia, and it really bothers me."

"Jenn, don't be upset, it won't do you any good."

Jenn looked like the kind of person who does as much as possible to take somebody out of an abyss but fails to do so.

After several hours waiting for Khrystal, she approached me to tell me that her mom called and she had to pick her up. I reached for her arm to stress that I had to tell her something very important, but

Khrystal pulled away violently. I stared at her as if saying *What's wrong with you? Why are you acting like that?*

Khrystal took her things off the table and, without saying a word, went to the door, while I shouted at her, "Khrystal, you don't want to get pregnant. Don't do that to catch Bob. That's the worst mistake you can make!"

Shocked, Khrystal turned back and angrily said, "I haven't intended to do that!"

"Well, think about it anyway, because it would be a big mistake."

She kept staring at me with a look of surprise, then turned around and left.

Days later, I went back to the gym. Khrystal approached me and asked me to stay away. She didn't want to have any kind of relationship with me. In the car on the way home, the spirits told me to turn back and try to convince her otherwise. I yelled at all the spirits to leave me alone, that they were wrong about trying to help a person who didn't have the slightest appreciateion for someone trying to help her, that her spiritual level was nonexistent, making everything harder and more complicated.

I got home, had some wine, walked out on the balcony, and asked the sky and the stars: "Why so much humiliation? She's a total nobody, a miserable hypocrite, a poor devil with no spiritual level. Where are you, God? Where is your justice? My intentions were good, and I've been rewarded with spite."

I was confused and stressed. The phone rang. It was my mother calling to tell me that Amasis needed to give me a message; I should call him as soon as I could. I ended the call with my mother and, without thinking too much about it, I called him.

"Hello?" he answered.

"Hello, Amasis, it's Julia. How are things going there? My mother gave me your message."

"Hi, Julia! Everything's fine here. Please, grab a piece of paper and a pen, I have to dictate some messages that are being sent from the spiritual world for you."

I grabbed a piece of paper and a pen. "I'm ready, Amasis ..."

"Your loved ones suggest that, from now on, you take some time to listen to God. He's at your door and calls you with different signals. If you manage to hear him, you only have to open the door so He can enter and dine with you. Fill yourself with faith in His guiding light, which shall bring order to your life. Whatever happens shall take place at the right time and in the right way. Learn from the past, make plans for the future, but live in the present. Instead of finding explanations on your own, trust the guide of the divine wisdom, let your home be a safe haven for you, your family, and your friends. God is in your home. Agree to live with relatives and friends in peace and love, so you accept God's presence. Keep in mind that God doesn't reside in places with indolence, criticism, judgment, incomprehension, greed, and lack of spirituality.

"Wash the feet of your neighbor, just like Jesus washed the feet of his disciples, and turn into what you are: a living example of Jesus. In order to do that, you only must become a compassionate and loving person in every circumstance. No resentments or fears. You have the power to establish harmony when there isn't any, and understanding when there is discontent. Say 'I trust in the mercy of God' every day. There are moments that you enjoy when you hear voices and see innocent faces that you like, and you feel a great inner peace. This isn't anything but the soft voice and the presence of the Holy Spirit, which relieves your soul and fills you with peace. Your evocations are like a divine love that resonates in your soul, whispers in a message of encouragement that your spiritual level is endorsed by God because He granted you that power so you can make a good use of it. Don't feel used and don't underestimate the power that you hold. Open your wings and many shall rejoice under your shadow. That's all, Julia, I hope that this message answers the questions that you've been asking to yourself, and gives you what you need to follow the pathway that has been created for you."

"Thanks, Amasis. Yes, the message answers my questions and much more. There's only one question that you don't answer: why me? I understood that I was an instrument for my family but, why for this ungrateful young woman with a dark soul and heart?"

"You will find that answer someday, but it's not for me to let you know. The answers come in different ways, not just through your earthly guide. Stay attentive and you will get your answer, one way or another."

"Okay, I know it's very late there. Have a good night, and thanks for all the things you do for me."

"Don't worry, Julia. It's my pleasure to be your earthly guide. I've learned many things with you. Have a great night, too."

When I hung up the phone, the voices of children walking around my room, and the sensation of tranquility and peace took over me once more. Besides, now I knew that it was the presence of the Holy Spirit.

Soon after I received the message, I got another very short one that said: "Child, with all the things you've done for me, I've earned the right to be on the light side. God bless you today and always. This mission has ended. Stay away from her, and let her go on with her life. It's time to move to new battles. There's just one more earthly mission left to pay the Karma that made you go back to the earthly world."

CHAPTER 6

Interlude

A FTER THE LAST MESSAGE received, I canceled my membership at that gym; I felt like I had lost my job. I thought, *maybe I need a long vacation before I start my next spiritual adventure. Just another Karma to be defeated.* I went to the mountains, bought a scratch pad, and started writing about any subject that my soul wanted to express. Without a specific order, I spontaneously recorded as many thoughts as would come to my mind:

Our nature defines us today, tomorrow, and always. When the values and concepts don't click between two or more people, the cohabitation and any type of relationship becomes finite, that is, it has a final point. I have seen and listened to great musical artists, and my body has shivered, feeling so much talent. We are impressed with all the things God can give us. I wondered, *what's for me? What can that gift be?*

When you find yourself in your worst moments, enjoy them in their entirety, hold and caress them. Without them, the greatness and the wonderful world that opens would never exist.

The beauty of every bad thing is the greatness of good. The roads open, opportunities come, dreams come true. Music is medicine for the mind and soul; a smile is a signal of hope. The musical notes remind you that you still can feel, inside of you, the magic that makes you live, the magic to be yourself, to be real, no matter the results.

Appreciating the talents in others is a gift. To be happy through the happiness of others is a gift.

A bad friendship makes you recognize the good ones and teaches you to cherish them.

Don't let anyone impose barriers on you, and don't impose barriers on yourself because you will find yourself locked in a time and space where you don't belong.

If you come to be something great, pursue what will lead you to get it with determination and persistence, only that way your life will have a meaning.

When you don't know which way to take, choose the one where your soul feels in peace and tranquility. In any of them, you will get far, and you'll be great in God's eyes because that's the way he wants it.

If there is a will, there is a way.

The indifference of others is like fire in your soul. You can't understand their actions and attitudes. You're not like them; you have a different nature; your essence is bathed in different scents. Don't try to understand them. Just be and let be.

Each person will harvest their own crop. Look around you for what was made for you.

We learn from our mistakes, even when they make us suffer too much.

Time: Everything happens in due time. Maybe we will not know the reasons why something happens today and not tomorrow, but that's not important. We only have to respect God's time. He, and only He, knows when we are ready to receive His blessings.

Our mental health can be appreciated in our ability to laugh at ourselves in the bad times.

Greed blinds those who haven't evolved, until the highest point of the human decline. It leaves them without a soul.

Questions: Why do we love so much those people that, one day, we have to forget and leave out of our lives? With our heart in our hands, we look for answers, patiently waiting for them to appear.

In this life, don't take love, appreciation, details, and attentions that you have received for granted. Cultivate and appreciate them. Those are the Lord's blessings.

Prayer: Father, give me the strength to change the things that I fear, to close old cycles and open new ones. Set me free from all my fears and help me to see the good in the bad.

I walked to one of the beautiful mountains of the town. Once more, inspiration took over me. I stopped by the side of the road to describe what I witnessed and felt:

I move among cold and white streets, surrounded by sad, dry, and shabby trees. The people around me are wrapped in their own world, automatic signals that block our human instinct, our behavior, our intention. Clouds of thoughts in my head, not knowing what they are, or what they will be. The music of this place fills me with imagination, wishful thinking that, someday, I'll be with the love of my life just like today, and everything around me will change its color. These dark and cold times of expectation will be illuminated by the lights of hope, which will come from the heavens.

You must work at something that you enjoy, even when you're not in your best moment. Change your way of being. If you want the world to change and be better, start with the change in you.

It continues: Give love; don't fear for your future; walk toward me; honor me; trust me. The tools shall be given to you.

There are many things that we believe to be important but aren't. It's sad to see how things that really matter that we should cultivate and give our time to, are confined in indifference and oblivion. This is the main reason for the existence of regret. When the years settle in the soul, that's when we manage to discover and listen to what was important from the real world, with the grace of recovering the lost time, and head for the pathway of truth.

What has walking an undiscovered road left for me if, at times, I think I know what hides inside of me? How many times have appearances deceived me and my life changed unexpectedly, inevitably, suddenly, and in most cases, irreversibly? My disappointments have been the same size of my expectations, and only by giving time to time, have I been able to go on the pathway. And the learning that came implicitly in these facts is my only consolation.

When the sun comes out, it's to advise that fortune will come to everyone in the same way. When the day is cloudy, it's to notify that it's necessary to rest. When it rains, it's time to reflect. When it snows, it's time to give in abundance. When it's too windy, it's time for love. When it's hot, it's time for consecration, and when it's too cold, it's time to heal and encourage.

Nothing replaces a look. Look for the eyes of everything that you want in life. That's where the soul appears, and the truth has been written.

Last night, before going back home, I had a strong desire to write about the city that had given me the chance to accomplish one of my missions in life and where I had harvested more spiritual and life experiences than I could've ever imagined. To the beat of Latin music, and while drinking a glass of wine, I took a piece of paper and a pen, and without thinking, I let my heart speak like this:

City of miracles, you have been the cradle
To let my dreams fly,
Becoming your voice
And offering my loyalty to you
Your wrapping landscapes
Have given me continuous warmth
In the cold streets of your walk.
In my clumsy days of loneliness
I remember and feel my homeland
Very close to my heart,
But your charming beauty
Already took a big part.
I can't stop loving you
Even if I wanted to,
I'm proud to be a part
Of your pretty residents,

To share my illusions
In your world of colors
Next to other authors.
Retouch your humble souls
To shape the nation
Sculpt it with my hands
That are filled with love
Your flag is in my chest
Your solemn hymn in my throat
Your History is in my mind
And your beauty in my sight
What else can I ask you?
What else can I give you?
How can I name you?
Land of freedom."

Back in the city, I got an e-mail from my mother. The subject was "Accept and allow to be led." The title of her message seemed interesting to me, so I opened it immediately.

Accept and allow to be led by your spiritual guide. She will guide you through the pathways that you'll walk to fulfill your valuable mission in the earthly world. Practice the conversion, perseverance, and forgiveness as a measure of acceptance as a missionary. God has crowned you with gifts to overcome obstacles that disturb your life and the lives of your loved ones. Once again, open the doors of your heart to everyone who requires it, and the doors of your house to whoever needs bread and shelter without expecting anything in exchange or rewards, because you will receive the Lord's infinite mercy forever, translated to abundance. You will reach the top and will not know how you climbed the stairs without being tired. You will reach out your hand to many, and many will reach out theirs to you; you only have to look up to the sky with humility and feel sure about accomplishing your noble mission. You wash the stains in your home, not in the presence of the neighbor, because they revert against you because you belong to the common core.

I called my mother as soon as I got home, to find out who sent this message to me. The message came from Amasis, and it was dictated to him by my great grandmother. I compared it with the first message that I received, and the word "conversion" was repeated. This time, I understood the message, but Khrystal's case was already finished, and there weren't any strange events happening, which made me think that it was something that might come in the future. Anyway, my father, John, had mentioned another mission and maybe this message was about that … that's what I thought at that moment.

CHAPTER 7

The Encounter II

I DECIDED TO ACCEPT A coworker's invitation to celebrate the city's annual ten-day summer fair. This fair was incredibly popular. People come from all over the world. I decided to go out to party.

When we were at the entrance, my coworker encountered a friend that she hadn't seen in years. They greeted each other effusively. Her friend was accompanied by a very handsome young man. We all introduced ourselves to each other, and I was interested in knowing what kind of relationship there was between my coworker's friend and the young man. We agreed to spend the day together at the fair. While there, we went to the restroom, and I took advantage of the moment to ask my coworker if she knew what kind of relationship her friend had with the young man. She told me that she had no idea.

"What's your friend's name again?"

"Alessandra."

When Alessandra came out of the restroom, I asked her, "Excuse me, Alessandra, but I don't recall your boyfriend's name."

"His name's Eduardo."

"Oh, Eduardo, it sounds like a Latin American name."

"Yes, he's from Costa Rica."

"And he was born here or came when he was a child? I mean, his English is very good. I would've never guessed that he's of Latin American origin, except for his name."

"He came when he was four years old. His family is very rooted to their culture, so he's been raised and educated practicing his customs, and that's one of the things that attracts me to him the most. You know, … I'm attracted to the fact that his customs are so different from mine, and I think it's very interesting."

"How long have you been together?"

"Almost two years now."

"Do you have any wedding plans yet?"

"No, not yet."

I could see in her sensational blue eyes that she wanted to marry Eduardo. Her tone of voice invited conversation. Upon first impression, her personality was really warm, which could make anybody feel comfortable. My friend Legna approached us and we stopped talking about Eduardo.

Alessandra and Legna recalled times when they had studied together in school and caught up on all the things that had happened over the years. Some stories were interesting and others a bit too bawdy for me. Once they were updated on what had happened since seeing one another last, they started talking more about the present. Alessandra had been in the city for a little while and was looking for a job. She had come after Eduardo with whom she was deeply in love. My friend asked for her resume at once. Apparently, she had worked in the Human Resources area before. She had seven years of experience, as well as a psychology degree. Dancing, talking, and drinking, the night was over too soon. Eventually, I gave up and became tired, so I decided to go home.

When I got to the front door of my house, I saw there was a bible. I took it, opened it, and read the page: Psalm 71, 17: Since my youth, God, you have taught me, and to this day I declare your marvelous deeds. The words "taught" and "marvelous" stuck in my mind. I couldn't make any sense out of it, but my recent experiences told me that something new was about to cross my path.

The visions and dreams appeared again. Now I could see airplanes in the air, fighting. A black-haired man with charming dark eyes cam to me and gave me a big hug. Sometimes I couldn't see anything at all; I just heard screams, bombs exploding, people communicating in a language I didn't understand, and I felt the suffering. The Nazi symbol started appearing everywhere. The symbols caught my attention, awakening sensations such as power, domination, and conquest.

I took several books from the public library and read about the Second World War. Most of the books that I read, focused on the suffering of the Jews and the persecution suffered by the Jehovah's Witnesses. Just as I was finishing one of the books, the doorbell rang. I rose from the sofa and opened the door. To my surprise, it was a Jehovah's Witness. A jovial and humble lady gave me the magazine of the week and suggested that we study the Bible together. Without thinking too much about it, I accepted.

From that day, Mrs. Dominga and I would sit and read the Bible together every Saturday morning. I was surprised by her knowledge of the Bible. She'd quote chapters and verses with precision and she moved back and forth between them very easily. In other words, she knew the Bible like the back of her hand. I loved to see her so dedicated, with so much faith, and taking the Word of the Lord to others.

I understood all of it and knew that the best way to open my heart to anyone in need of bread and shelter was through the study of the word. I needed to serve them as a consolation and instruct them. To me, in those moments, the bread was the consolation that they would find in the word by themselves.

With Mrs. Dominga, I learned many things. Still, several of them were related to her religion, and I didn't share her opinion sometimes. For example, I could never see or interpret what they understand about blood transfusion in the Bible.

After four weeks, I was taking the elevator at work, and when the doors opened, I saw Alessandra standing in front of me. "Hi, how are you?" I said, pleased to see her.

"Fine, I'm very happy."

"What are you doing here?"

"Legna got me a job as a talent recruiter."

"That's great news! When did you start?"

"I had my first day yesterday."

"Wonderful!" Then I understood why Legna couldn't join me for lunch. She'd must've eaten with Alessandra. "Do you have plans for lunch today?" I asked.

"No, not yet," she answered.

"I know a very good Italian restaurant nearby."

"Sure, what time do you want to meet?"

"What if you stop by my office on the eleventh floor around 11 AM? It's 1131."

"Ok, I'll see you later. She left in the elevator.

At 11 AM, Alessandra showed up in my office and we went to eat. I tried to contact Legna to join us, but she hadn't come to work so I left her a message. We walked a couple blocks to the restaurant. I noticed that Alessandra seemed different. "Is there something wrong, Alessandra?

"No, I'm fine. I'm just happy with my new job."

We arrived at the restaurant, sat down, and ordered some drinks. Silence prevailed while we read the menu to see what we could eat. The young waitress came to take our orders and told us that it would take about fifteen minutes.

I kept feeling like there was something strange about Alessandra, but I didn't want to insist on it. I didn't know her well enough and she might be offended. Instead, I dedicated myself to getting to know her better.

"Alessandra, that's an Italian name?

"Yes," she answered. "My father was Italian and his name was Alessandro. He gave me the female version of his name."

"It's a pretty name. What about your mom?"

"She's from here."

"Do you have any brothers or sisters?"

"I have two brothers, but no sisters. I'd say Legna was like my sister for those years we were in school."

"Yes, Legna is an amazing person. I really appreciate her a lot."

"And you?" Alessandra inquired.

"I also have two brothers. And one sister. By the way, you really remind me of her."

"In what sense?"

"You don't bear a resemblance, but the two of you are very sociable, and it's comfortable to talk and hang out with you."

"Okay, nice to know." Alessandra said. "Where are you from? I notice that you have an accent, but I can't tell from where."

"I speak Spanish like Eduardo, your boyfriend. I'm from Venezuela.

Immediately, Alessandra began to speak to me in Spanish.

The waitress brought our lunch. I was very hungry, so I spent the rest of the time busy with my food. We asked for the check and split it. We walked back to the office.

That night, I sat on the balcony of my house with my cell phone while I texted my sister and enjoyed a cup of coffee. Suddenly, I began to have visions. I saw a man in a uniform. He was a German fighter pilot, very handsome, with a mustache and deep, teary eyes. He was holding somebody's hands and kissed them with an enviable tenderness. I experienced sensations with these situations: My heart felt sorrow. The visions disappeared, but the sensations didn't. The pain in my heart was from a deep feeling of loss.

Then I started feeling the presence of a woman who repeated words: "I miss you," and hugged me, encouraging me to hug her back. Finally, I could see her eyes: they were a blue, similar to Alessandra's. I didn't really know what to do, so I lay down on the bed and hugged the entity in torment.

Weeks later, when I saw Alessandra again, I looked at her eyes more closely. To my surprise, they were exactly like the ones of the entity that I had sheltered the other night. We talked about meeting at her place, since her mother and siblings were coming to celebrate Family Day, and she knew I was alone in the city. Somebody whispered in my ear that she had something very valuable for me inside of her. I turned to look at Alessandra again, and asked, "Alessandra, is everything okay?"

"Julia, you've already asked me that several times. Why?"

"I don't know, there's something different about you." Legna was with us so I turned to her and asked, "Legna, do you see something different in her?"

Looking, she replied, "No, I see her just as usual. But Julia, what do you see?" She leaned back in her chair and looked at me, daring me to give the reasons why I felt that way, reasons I couldn't describe.

"I don't know, it's not bad, but I can't decipher it yet."

At the office, I started trying to figure it out, until, finally something told me: *Alessandra is pregnant*. After that, I waited until she wanted to tell me.

About fifteen days passed when Alessandra called me. "Julia, can you come to my office? I need to show you something."

I wasn't doing anything, so I went up to the 21ˢᵗ floor where Alessandra worked. She opened her e-mail and showed me an echogram, then just looked at me and smiled. Her face and eyes shone with high intensity as she exclaimed, "I'm pregnant!"

I got up from my seat and gave her a big hug. "I'm so happy for you, Alessandra. Who knows?"

"My family, Eduardo, of course, Legna and other friends."

"How did he react to the news?"

"Very good," Alessandra answered.

"Do we have a wedding, then?"

"No, not yet."

That weekend, I met with Alessandra and her family. Thank goodness Alessandra extended that invitation to me, or I would have spent another family day alone, eating ice cream at home. I felt good surrounded by people filled with family spirit.

From that day, my relationship with Alessandra became closer. I didn't know why I started to develop an overprotective relationship with her. I took care of her during her pregnancy as if the child she was expecting were mine. My attachment to her and her baby wasn't normal, so I stayed away every once in a while. I didn't like to feel like that. I was suffocated by the idea of her not being happy, of suffering, that something might happen to her or the baby.

Several months later, the baby was born, and she named him Lucas. It was all happiness – Lucas was beautiful and healthy, and attracted the attention of everybody. He was like a movie star. Alessandra dedicated herself completely to Lucas. Several times, we took him to parks, restaurants, or we'd just meet at her house or mine to talk and play with Lucas.

As soon as Lucas was six months old, Alessandra began to travel to different places every month. I was happy for her and Lucas, but sometimes I'd go more than a month without seeing Lucas, and that made me very sad. Still, I never wanted to let her know. I recognized that my feelings were a bit strange, and I didn't want to lose her friendship and the chance to be in contact with Lucas. Then there was a moment ... in which things escalated, so I decided that it was a good time to contact my earthly guide to find an explanation. Instead of calling him at his home, I decided to catch a flight to Venezuela to talk to him in person.

Once I'd arrived back home in Venezuela, I spent almost a week visiting with relatives and friends. As soon as everybody returned to their regular businesses, I contacted Amasis and went to his house to visit him. "The things that are happening to me are very strange, and I don't feel comfortable," I told him.

"Let's see, kid ... tell me what's wrong ..."

Then I told him about Alessandra, Lucas, and all the visions that I'd had.

"There might be a connection between Alessandra, Lucas, and your visions," Amasis said. "You must try to clear your mind, so you can connect with your consciouness. The answers will be there and you will also find the connections there. It seems that the events happened during the Second World War. If you are somehow involved in the events that happened, we could say that it's another mission. Find the connection, identify what you're expected to do, and do what you're told to, no matter how crazy or out of this world it sounds to you. Let me ask you something else, Julia. Have you felt the presence of Alessandra's soul looking for shelter in you, in times that seem to be of sadness?"

"Yes! That happens very often. I feel it and even see it sitting or reclining with a sad and anguished demeanor."

"And what do you do in those moments, Julia?"

"Although it seems crazy, I hug her and whisper 'shushushu' in her ear ... and I caress her."

Amasis smiled and continued, "You can go now. Trust your heart, it is noble and will help you to overcome any setbacks."

"Thanks, Amasis." I got up, gave him a big hug, and said goodbye.

Back home, I talked about the whole thing with my mother and my nanny. They were as surprised and confused as me. My mother's imagination flew; she tried to draw conclusions and create stories. I told her to wait until I had more information after I'd connected with my consciouness. I only had a few days left with my family and friends in Venezuela, so I put the whole thing about Lucas and Alessandra aside.

Once back in my northern home, I began to meditate. For a moment, I fell completely asleep. I saw the airplanes and Alessandra's eyes again, this time in a much quicker motion. Once again, everything was happening out of sequence, very messy. This time, I saw a mirror. I approached it to see my reflection – who I was, what I looked like. To my surprise, I was a German fighter pilot. I turned around and saw the woman with Alessandra's eyes dressed in white clothes. With great joy, she opened her arms and said, "You came back to me at last." I took her hands, feeling their delicate softness. "Our son has been born again," she said. "Go and take care of him in the earthly world. Go and help me to build a life. Difficult times will come to me and make me suffer. Don't let me go on the wrong path; seed hope in me and guide me to my real love."

"Who is your real love?"

The woman disappeared and I immediately woke up all sweaty.

Months after this dream, Alessandra called to tell me that she would be leaving home to live separate from Eduardo because she could no longer stand his infidelities and his domestic, drug, and alcohol abuse. I remembered the message I received about the difficult times that would come to Alessandra. Quickly, I scheduled an appointment with her. We agreed to meet at our favorite breakfast place the following Saturday.

That Saturday morning, my friend was not the same person I'd met before. A feeling of frustration arose inside me. It was obvious that her relationship with Eduardo had broken her deeply. I tried to come up with topics that could relax her and, of course, we talked about the funniest and most interesting of Lucas's adventures as well. The morning flew by in their company. After we finished our meals, we went for a walk in the mall. Then they had to go and I did too.

The next day, I felt an urgency to let her know my thoughts, so I sent her an email:

There is not a perfect relationship, but being able to recognize and end a relationship that does not add anything positive to you as a human being, is a great achievement. Don't let his shadow follow and overtake you; don't allow frustration to cloud your soul and propel you down the wrong path. Remember who you really are: a confident woman, independent, sociable, open to new ideas, determined, and with high self-esteem. Eduardo was not the man of your life, he was just a lesson learned in your life. After this experience, you will be able to discover and appreciate fully the love and company of the man that God has reserved for you. Don't give up on yourself, hope is a key element in your life. Hope is waiting for you, just waiting for you to wake up out of that lethargy where you are trapped. Your real love will knock at your door when you least expect it, and I will be around you to confirm it.

With love,
Julia

On Monday morning, Alessandra called me. I was really happy with what she said. She was determined to end her cycle with Eduardo and open herself to God's will.

At work, I was insanely busy and my communication with Alessandra stopped for a while. I kept an eye on them through Facebook. A few months passed and Alessandra called me at my office; she wanted to get together to talk. My work pace had slowed down a bit, so I had time to meet with her. I accepted her invitation to have supper and suggested a pub close to my office.

"Hi, how are you?" I asked her as I arrived at the table where she was already sitting.

"Everything is good on my side," she replied with a big smile on her face.

"Do you want to order drinks to start or do you want to go to the food menu right away?" I asked.

"I am starving, let's order the food," Alessandra replied.

"Hahaha, okay, I know what I want already. What about you? Do you know?"

"No, I don't know what I want; this is my first time here. I'm not familiar with the menu, what do you recommend?"

"Anything is good here! Right now I love the seafood platter."

"Ok, let's do that one."

"What do you want to drink, Alessandra?"

"A lemonade."

"Are you sure? What about a white wine?"

"No, I am good. Lemonade is good today."

"Okay." I motioned for the waitress.

"Yes, what have you ladies decided to have today?

"Two lemonades and two seafood platters," I replied. "How long do you think that will take?" I asked, checking my watch.

"Around fifteen minutes," the waitress replied.

"Okay, thanks."

She took the menus and quickly walked away.

"What do you want to tell me? I am really curious here," I said in a funny way.

"Hahaha, well, I believe I have found my true love, as you told me I would."

"Awesome, great news, why didn't you want to have the wine instead then? We have a reason to celebrate!"

"Haha, we can cheer with our lemonades," she said.

"Let me ask you some questions," I said.

"Okay, ask away." She leaned toward me.

"First of all, what is his name?"

"Sean."

"How good is his relationship with your immediate family?"

"Is very good. Lucas is a little bit jealous of him. Now that he understands that Lucas's behavior is part of the process of adjustment, he has been very patient with him. He also has a very good relationship with my dad too. He loves them all—"

I interrupted, "Is he spoiling Lucas?"

"No, he plays and pleases him once in a while, but he demands Lucas maintain discipline and good behavior most of the time. I dare to say that he does a better job than Lucas's biological father. I believe Sean is an excellent father for my son."

"Does he have a job?" I asked.

"Yes, he is working currently for the oil and gas industry. He has a good position, and he is very responsible, a hard worker, and very knowledgeable about what he does."

"Do you guys share the same interests?"

"Yes, we have many things in common, we both love sports and outdoors activities."

"Do you love really love him?"

"Yes, I do."

The food and drinks arrived and we toasted with our drinks for the new person in Alessandra's life.

Suddenly, I heard a whisper in my ear: *Sean is her true love, tell her.* Without hesitation I told her, "Alessandra, before we start our meal, I want to let you know, Sean is your true love in this life. Don't let him go, don't waste this opportunity, he is the one."

A brigh light shone from her stunning blue eyes, blinding my sight. She hugged me warmly, and we dug into our meals, enjoying, with ecstasy, the mix of flavors.

I felt my mission with Alessandra was over. She was able to find stability in her life, her true love, a person to make plans with and to rebuild and create a home for Lucas. In front of one of the city's rivers, I asked to hear the whole story. Somehow, I wanted to relive the events. Something told me that, even with all the bad things that might have happened, real and unconditional love triumphed in that story; I wanted to feel it again.

CHAPTER 8

Memories

WEEKS LATER, THE MEMORIES became more vivid, tangible, and contained more meaning. I took a pen and a piece of paper, and I wrote the story of my past life with Alessandra. I could connect the random points and create a passage even though there were some gaps and inaccuracies of what that past-life relationship was.

In my memories, he was injured in one of the many battles that he'd fought. When he woke up, found himself in a very clear and spacious place, but with groans and cries of pain prevailing. He couldn't move his neck or remember exactly how he got there. He must have lost conscience for a long time.... A warm voice, that he'll never forget, resonated in his ears. For some strange reason, he couldn't understand what it said. He panicked at the thought that he was at the hands of my enemies. He tried to calm down, and in a matter of seconds began to understand what it was telling him:

"Sir, you're in the hospital. My name is Alina. You've got a very serious injury in your neck. Try not to move too much."

He answered, "Ok, fine, I can understand you now. Is it possible that the other people stop making so much noise? I'm really dazed with so many cries and whines."

"They have a lot of pain and our supplies are not enough. Many of the patients suffer their pain without anesthesia. We are doing as much as we can for them."

"How did I get here? My name is Johann, I'm a Luftwaffe fighter pilot."

"I don't know how you got here, Johann, or what happened to you. I only receive the patients and give first aid to them. Some of your superiors will show up soon, and they will clarify all your questions.

"I'm very thirsty," I told Alina. She poured some water into a cloth, and gave it to him to suck since I couldn't move my neck.

"I have to see other patients, but if you need anything else, ring this bell."

"Thanks for all your care; you have a big heart. This work you do mustn't be easy. I've been awake for only fifteen minutes and I'm going nuts already."

Alina smiled at his comment, looked at him tenderly, and left.

Johan closed his eyes trying to sleep again ... but the cries wouldn't let him. For a moment, he thought of Alina: her voice, her stare, the subtle and beautiful way she cared for him, and managed to fall asleep.

I didn't remember anything else about our meeting. I couldn't see or remember how we came to establish a relationship. I only saw myself as a pilot in an airplane, fighting in the sky, arriving at different places, and in each of the visions there was a woman who looked at me with love in her eyes. I didn't feel any kind of commitment to anything or anybody. I never reflected on, or thought about, what I was doing. To me, it was just the way he had to live: no regrets and not judging or censoring his actions.

Still, after he met Alina, for the first time ever, he thought about somebody in his times of loneliness during his battles, and when he thought he was doing justice and defending his country. Alina's eyes were fixed in his soul. He'd dream of them almost every day, and her voice remained with him. She awoke a different reason in him to battle. He wanted her to be safe, live well, and be happy. He didn't want to lose the freedom that he enjoyed, but the need to be with her and love her got more and more fixed in his soul.

It was then when he decided to look for her. He arrived at the hospital and there was Alina, dedicated to serving others and being their biggest hope.

"Alina!" She turned around and looked at him with surprise. Her white clothes were stained with blood, as were her hands and part of her face. The man she was taking care of looked really bad. There was blood all over the place. Johan looked at the floor and he was standing in a pool of blood. "I need to talk to you."

Alina looked around the place and told him, "This isn't the right time. Let me finish here and then I'll see you. Can you wait for me in the central courtyard?"

He nodded.

He waited for her for hours. It was already getting dark when she showed up.

"Hello, Johann. How have you been?"

"Fine. I'm sorry I burst in the way I did, but I needed you."

"I don't get it."

"Me neither. Since I met you, things have been different for me."

"In what sense?"

He smiled, a bit embarrassed. He was really afraid that she'd reject him. "In every sense. Look, I'm a strong man, a warrior ... but you've made me feel and see a part of me that I didn't know."

"I had a very hard day today," Alina replied. "I don't know if I'm in the best mood to talk about these kinds of things. Can we talk another day?"

Unfortunately, patience wasn't one of his virtues, and he blurted, "I really need to know many things today, I came here to get some answers and I won't leave without them."

"What you've said so far sounds a bit complicated. I just want to be in the best mood to give you the best answer to your questions—"

"Do you feel something for me, that it's not just friendship or affection?" Johan interrupted.

"Yes, Johann. I think about you during the day, and each time I've asked my heart if you're something special that God brought into my life. It says yes."

He was speechless for a while. He couldn't believe that so many hours thinking of what to say, how to say it and how Alina would react, would translate into just seconds. He felt a huge happiness, and there was no more fear of being heartbroken. Johan went closer and caressed her soft, delicate face. Slowly, he got closer and kissed her, taking her upper lips and squeezing them between his. He felt some sort of sting in his heart and his breathing shortened. Everything was perfect: the scents, the colors, and the wind that wrapped around the moment and held it.

Suddenly, my memories faded away and I couldn't remember more of that moment between Johann and Alina that day. Due to circumstances, Alina and Johann couldn't live their lives together in a normal relationship. They barely saw each other, and, each time they separated, only God knew if they'd see each other again. This made them live every second they shared as if it were their last moment together. Not knowing what the future held for them in a warring world, and asking if there even was a future for them at all, made them embrace the present. It was the only thing they could be sure about. They just totally gave themselves to each other. They didn't make plans, didn't promise anything to each other, and didn't raise expectations.

They just enjoyed and thanked God for allowing love, understanding, and passion in times of war.

Months later, more visions and conversations between Alina and Johann came to my mind. Johann would tell me some things: that Alina can play the violin; she learned to play it when she was very young, and she said that all her life, the violin had helped her to go through tragic, sad, and even happy times. The notes and the subtle sounds that came out of the violin translated into messages for her.

One of the many nights they spent together, enjoying the starry skies and the fire of their hearts, craving for thrills and consolation for all the inhuman things that they found and dealt with every day, Alina played one of her favorite pieces. Johan didn't know what to think or say. He couldn't find a way to describe all the significance and all the sensations growing in him that moment. He looked up to the sky and felt small drops of rain falling on them, and told her:

"The angels from heaven are crying with joy. Come with me, let's seal our life together before the Heavenly Court. Accept my virtues and defects. Take me in the good and the bad, forgive me when I mortally wound your heart and soul inadvertently, when my selfishness takes over me and tries to take me away from your arms. Beat the evil and the treason with unconditional love. Let your eyes only look at me tenderly and passionately. Let your lips only kiss my lips, and let the muse and your musical prowess guide me to find you wherever you are, here and any other place where I can be when I have to go someday. Let your belly be the bosom of all the things that I feel and have felt for you since our paths crossed. Let your breasts give me the nourishment that I need to feel loved and thus be able to carry out all the tasks that I'm required to do."

Alina didn't say a word. In light of the silence, Johan opened his eyes, took her hands and kissed them, stroked her hair, and kissed her on her cheek. For quite a while, they stayed looking at each other, face to face. Her eyes sparkled like a sky of stars, but no words came from her mouth. Finally, she broke the silence, "You ask for big things that my heart is willing to give. You ask my soul to be your guide, your truth, and your reason, and my soul is willing to be always there for you. The song that I just played warns me that something big is coming for both of us. Our real big moment is about to come, and I'm glad to know that your feelings are here with me, and that they are only for me."

Alina caressed his hair, and they kissed until they became only one. The white sheets witnessed a beautiful and passionate episode in their lives.

Her words remained with him. He wasn't sure what she meant when she said that something big would come for us; it could be much bigger than what he was already feeling for her.

Alina was a strong person, and she was kind and sensitive at the same time. The idea of seeing her unhappy each time he had to leave her really bothered him. He felt that, somehow, he left a space and a feeling of loss in her heart, and he hated that. At times, he started wondering how could he quit on everything and never stay away from her life. He thought about deserting. He didn't care about the complications or implications that this would bring to him. Together, they could escape from everything and everyone and live a normal life in any other place.

While he was thinking about this, he noticed how much he had changed. Before meeting Alina, Johan never would have thought about doing something like that, but he realized that everything he had pursued in life before meeting Alina made no sense. he had defended his country for years. He had been the hero in hundreds of battles. He had seen the enemy die in front of him. He had to learn to live with the memory of watching how life abandoned the bodies of his victims.

It was something scary to witness the last breath of his enemies of war. Many times, they'd asked for forgiveness, many times they begged for mercy and he hadn't listened. He'd just done what he was trained to do. He'd forgotten they were just like him, that somebody loved them and waited for them, just like Alina waited for him.

In his deep moments of reflection, he'd desperately look for some feeling of peace and joy after all those deeds, and he found only sadness and strong regrets. Instead, now, everything that Alina made him feel was joy and peace. On a full moon night, Johan wrote a poem for Alina. Her eyes were what he loved most about her. They were charming and deep, as if her soul escaped through them.

> *When I look into your eyes*
> *I feel a great pleasure*
> *I have seen them before*
> *I have wanted them too*
> *Blue as the sea*
> *Intense as the sun*
> *Bright as the moon*
> *Ideal for love*
> *and the loving gaze from your eyes dominates me*
> *They cause a thousand smiles in me*
> *They follow me and take care of me*
> *In my deepest dreams*
> *I want to draw your stare*
> *And have it with me forever*
> *Until I have to go.*

That same night, after they had dinner and he read his poem to her, Alina took a picture, that she had in her night table, out of the frame and gave it to him. "I want you to take it with you everywhere. I want you to always remember me as much as I remember you."

"Hahahaha, I don't need to have a picture of you to have you in my mind all the time. You should rather give me the secret to getting a little bit of you out of me because sometimes I feel that I am suffocating when I'm not with you and my mind puts you as a priority over myself."

Alina smiled, and her face blushed and brightened. "I have something important to tell you."

"What is it? You sound very serious and happy at the same time."

"Honestly, I'm afraid of what your reaction might be. I know that you love me, and I know that your feelings are sincere, but I have no idea if you are ready for the reality presented to us."

He didn't know what to think. He had no idea of what it was about, but Alina's words managed to worry him. He held her hands and said, "Anything you want to tell me, please, feel safe. I don't want fear to be an obstacle between you and me."

Alina took a deep breath, look directly into his eyes, and told him through tears, "I'm pregnant. I'm expecting your baby."

Johann was speechless. He let go of Alina's hands and sat on the edge of the bed, turning his back on her. Johann thought that it was something big, that he loved her as much as his future child, but it wasn't the best moment. He turned around, hugged her, held her hair, took her face gently in his hands and kissed her tenderly on her forehead and told her what he had been thinking. "I feel happy, there's nothing I want more than being with you and having children, but Alina, this is not the best time for it. The war is not over yet. Our future and that of our country is uncertain; I can't take care of you, of me, of our country, and, now, a child. The circumstances are unfavorable, and I want a world of opportunities, of safety and health for my child, but I have to build it first."

Alina listened to him. She knew that, in a way, he was right, but she didn't understand why after so many loving words and so many demonstrations of commitment, he reacted to the reality of a baby with so much logic. What were his true feelings before the reality? Did they exist or not? Faced with so much confusion, Alina didn't want to talk about it anymore. She turned around, lay down on the bed, and told him, "I don't want to talk about it anymore."

"Alina, I have to leave tomorrow. I think that we need to talk; it can't wait for another day. We don't even know what *another day* means to us."

"Your position is very clear. In this reality it's not the best moment for you."

"That's right, it isn't, but I do love our future child. I love you very much. Please, don't ignore me, I don't want to go tomorrow and leave you upset or sad. I want to say goodbye to each other as usual. I need you, I need the warmth of your body, and I need your hugs and kisses."

Alina turned around, hugged him and kissed him, and they spent the night holding each other.

At dawn, Johann decided to desert the army. This would be his last mission; he would return to Alina forever and would look for a way to give her and his son a decent life. Johann didn't want his son to go through all the things he had gone through, or do all the things he had to do. He arrived at the base, put Alina's picture in his pocket close to his heart, and went on his mission.

I don't have too many memories from this episode. I've only been able to visualize falling from the airplane. Johann was taken down. He heard people yelling and celebrating around him. Alina's picture slighty visible, sticking out of his pocket. One of the captors took it, laughed, and showed it to the others. He didn't understand what they were saying. Most likely it wasn't his language, or he was scared, and his nerves wouldn't let him understand, as had happened to him before when he met Alina.

One of the imprisioners took the picture and started licking Alina's face, and then they burst into laughter. The young man who was closer to him, raised his gun and put it against Johan's head. In that moment, Johan remembered his whole life up until his last night with Alina. He asked God to help him; he wanted to meet his son; he wanted to see Alina again. In the eyes of the man pointing the gun, he could see the look of death, the stare of someone who had no mercy, just like he had been several times. He felt what his victims had felt, and then he pleaded, "Please, spare my life. I have a wife and a son to take care of. Have mercy on me."

I only heard the sound of the gun. And, in a few seconds, Johan was out of his body looking down at it. There was no soul in his eyes. The man had pulled the trigger and taken his life immediately. His soul wandered for a while and didn't know how to get to Alina. He didn't know what sign to follow, so he started walking around places that he had never seen before, nothing was familiar. His soul wandered for days, until his father appeared. His father took his hand and assured him, "Everything's fine now, there's nothing to worry about. We'll take care of everything. Come with me; you have to pull through. You'll get explanations and you'll be given new chances under other conditions."

Johan didn't understand any of what his father was saying. "But, what will happen to Alina?"

"She'll go on with her life. Your child will be born, and it will be a boy. He will take care of her, and she'll never find another love in her life. To her, you're not dead. To her, you just never returned because, basically, you didn't want the responsibility of having a child."

"But that's not true."

"I know, son. Trust in God's will. His father repeats. You will be given a new chance under other conditions."

This was the last thing that I remembered of my life as Johann.

CHAPTER 9

The Awakening

I HADN'T NOTICED THAT A long time had passed and my life had been limited, so to speak. I had to help people I had hurt in my past lives. I felt very good knowing that my two main missions had been accomplished.

There was some sort of heaviness in my soul, so I decided to take a few days off at the beach and made sure to be as isolated as I could from everything. I had the huge need to be in touch with nature. Those were the most beautiful mornings that I'd ever seen in my life. The sunset, the beach, the sand, the trees, the sea, the waves, the moon, the stars. Everything was in harmony with my being.

The birds were singing at my window to greet me in the morning; they were very funny, always singing, flying, enjoying, without working hours to comply with and no worries. It was then when I understood that there was something awakening inside of me.

At times, I thought that I had already been in a place even more beautiful than the one I had in front of me. The sensations of peace, happiness, compassion, understanding and unconditional love that I felt while I stared at the beauty around me weren't new because my soul had experienced them in another moment.

Walking by the shore, I found three stones of different sizes, and they fascinated me. It was like love at first sight! I named the first stone "the stone of wisdom." It was the smallest. I named the second, of medium size, "the stone of peace," and I named the biggest of them "the stone of happiness." I thought that, by obtaining wisdom, it would be much easier to build a wall of peace that we can trespass and pass to others, and achieve a total happiness for all.

Then I took the smallest stone and washed it. The breeze gently stroked my hair and the sun burned my skin. Once I finished washing the stone of wisdom, I went back to the little house where I was staying. I filled the bathtub with water, poured in bath salts, lit some scented candles and got in. I took the stone in my hands and started kissing it. I was surprised by the tenderness that I kissed it with, and by all the sensations of plenitude that the stone made me feel.

About thirty minutes passed, and I began to see some white doors opening and a bright light illuminated my feet. A man came to my bathtub, and told me, "This stone is a gift from God. Your obedience and good heart have allowed you to remember and be in touch with your own home. Soon you'll enjoy the job you held before going to the earthly world to accomplish your missions."

I heard a very loud sound and woke up. I had fallen asleep. There was a bold thunderstorm outside and it was raining heavily. I got out of the bathtub, dried myself and my stones, and put them on my nightstand.

All these experiences told me that the heaviness that I felt in my soul was because it was tired of wandering away from home. Although my missions gave me immense satisfaction, maybe it was about time to go back. I only lamented that the physical love of a man probably wasn't going to be a part of my life.

Completely rejuvenated, I went back to the city. I felt that my first day of work was very heavy. It cost me so much to get out of bed early, after having had the freedom to do whatever I wanted. Now I had to go back to the routine and to do things, like it or not. For the first time, I felt that this entire work thing didn't give me much satisfaction. I faced these kinds of feelings, and I hoped they'd be temporary. The days passed by slowly and things got worse. Each day, I felt less interest in the idea of going to work. I desperately tried to find a balance. My feelings were one of the things that concerned me the most. I started rejecting the idea of being in the earthly world. Everything stopped being important. I didn't care about my job, and I didn't achieve anything in it. Internally, something told me that the things I had fought for, and for which I had given all of me to reach them, weren't really worth it. I started going to the park during lunch hour to be in touch with nature.

Nature had become my escape. I took refuge in the trees, the river, the winds and the park's grass and I covered myself up with their peace and wisdom. Each day I went to watch nature. Once again, I had the impression that, somehow, I had watched all that beauty before, but in another dimension. I began to develop different ideas. I wished that we could all live in complete harmony, that we would help each other all the time. I imagined a world with no boundaries; a world that belonged to all of us the same; where there would only be love, compassion, and mercy; a world of equality, where each one of us would be happy for the wonderful experiences lived by others; where all the positive events and the important qualities ruled. I felt a frustration every time there was injustice in the environment of love and compassion. I didn't find any answers even though I was looking for my guide's counseling. There was a reason for this, but I didn't know what it was either.

My birthday arrived and I started getting several messages. One of them was to look for one of my friends so she could baptize me in the river. On my way to her house, I thought that I should tell her to dress all in white. That was one of the requirements, and I was already completely dressed in white. To my surprise, when I arrived at my friend's house and she opened the door, she was fully dressed in white. I didn't need to tell her anything. That increased the faith of following the messages sent by my guide.

The words I had to say to my friend when I was immersed in the river's waters were "Lord, receive your daughter" and so she did. The other received messages were more related to my mission in life, my work was only an instrument to reach the people that I had to motivate to change their lives. I shouldn't stay in the same place for a long time; I had to move in order to cover more ground. Nature would have all the answers for me to connect with others and to ensure my physical and mental health and the physical and mental health of every soul that I'd touch. The changes, no matter how small, were going to create big differences. It was a day of renewal and chance to re-encounter my path.

As the days passed, I found myself more and more dedicated to a different life, but I didn't find a way to make others understand which things really mattered and that we had to ensure during our time in this world.

I kept experiencing the connection to the other world. One beautiful moonlit night, my spiritual guide sat on my bed, and I was very happy for his presence and anxious to get answers from him.

"You've already seen and experienced several things," my guide said.

"Yes, and I really appreciate everything. I believe that what I've seen and perceived belongs to the other world, not here, where evil reigns. I'd like to know if I'm right, and how this has been possible."

"There is a physical mind and the consciouness. Your consciouness is loaded with memories of the spiritual world where you belong, but the physical mind doesn't allow you to have access to these memories. As soon as you turn the physical mind off, you have access and remember things. Have you refused to live on Earth?"

"Yes, lately," I answered.

"Why?"

"Because nothing is like I feel it should be."

"And how do you feel it should be?"

"Living in complete harmony and helping each other, instead of competing. I believe that each one of us has a talent, and it's not the talent that really matters, but what we do with it, and that is just putting it to use for the service of the others."

"Yes, that's right. Now you feel it and think about it because you have started remembering your own world. But you won't find that on Earth. Your soul is good, and if you have already begun to remember, it might be good because you've learned to control your mind, or it might be that your world is calling you."

"Does that mean that I'll die in the earthly world in order to go home?"

"Yes, it is possible."

"Wait, … you don't know? I thought you could see the future."

"The future changes constantly with your decisions and with events that affect it and make it change," my guide answered. "At first, it may be that you were meant to die of old age, but if your soul connects and asks to go back, all of that can change, and you'll go home earlier."

"What's the point of earthly life then?" I asked him.

"It's your chance to improve your soul so you can reach higher levels and be purified."

"Besides remembering, what other benefit is given by the connection?" I asked.

"You are allowed to recognize God's laws. And you have a better discernment of good and evil."

"You talk about levels. What's that?"

"There are several levels. The first levels are the shadows, where evil dwells. There is an intermediate level, and then the last are the levels of light, where good lives."

"What will happen to me when I die?"

"Well, you call it dying because that's the way your physical mind understands it. Nobody dies. Everybody goes home. Depending on their actions in life, they will go back to the low or high levels of the spiritual world."

"If I've done wrong sometimes, what can I do to make up for it?"

"Repent from the heart. Bear in mind, the most important thing is not the acts themselves, but your intentions. Before doing something, always ask yourself what is pushing you to do it. If they are bad things such as hatred, envy, and revenge, then don't do them. If it is love, compassion, and willingness to serve others, you can be sure that God will appreciate it. Now, don't do the things just because you want to earn a good position at home, because that translates into a selfish act, something you do for yourself instead of for somebody else."

"Will I see my family?"

"Of course, but they must be at your same level to enjoy more of them."

"Who will come for me?"

"I don't know that, but there are many people who love you and take care of you. Any of them could. Humans will never stop looking for answers and ask thousands of questions to their guides. They tend to complicate everything with their doubts, which always prevail in their hearts. Open yourself to the only truth: the Earth is not your home. Learn, but don't push yourself to get anything that is not the purification of your soul. That's the only thing that matters in your transition through the earthly life."

CHAPTER 10

The Park

I KEPT VISITING THE PARK to connect with nature. One day, while I was walking, a strong and melodious voice caught my attention. The voice, to the strum of the guitar's melody, invited me to search for where it was coming from. When I got closer, I saw a very good-looking young man playing a song. I sat on a bench near the young man to listen to him. While I was looking at him, I wondered, *Why would he be here, in the walkways of a park, expressing his art in exchange for coins? How come nobody has been able to value the talent that lies, lives, and vibrates soundly inside of him?*

His eyes were piercing, his hands mastered the strings of his guitar, and his voice touched my soul and wove millions of thoughts into my mind with each verse and chorus. My body proved weak when faced with so much magic, and yet I didn't want to get away.

With the sound of his angelic voice, the sky cried with joy, and it started raining. The young man's mood changed: his face showed discontent. For him, the rain was a hindrance, nothing beautiful and worth enjoying. It wasn't a good companion for his purpose. He stopped playing and singing. Arrogance oozed through his pores, and the scenery was completely dissonant. The magic and vibes in my body stopped flowing and fear took over. I thought, *Am I too close to him? Should I have stepped back to a few benches away, or maybe gone back to do my daily tasks?*

The young man continued with an increasingly aggressive attitude, and his vocabulary became obscene. A young woman in exercise clothing walking by, who seemed entertained by his outburst, was verbally attacked by the young man. I really didn't understand his outrage at the rain. Like everything in life, the rain was temporary. The sun would come out again soon, and luck would go back in his favor. Obviously, the young man didn't feel the same way. Maybe I should have gotten closer to him and expressed my perception of the situation ... perhaps my vision might have helped him to adopt a better attitude. But, fear was still taking over me.

I just kept staring at the young man from my perch on the bench. For a moment, I was so fascinated with the environment filled with colors and conflicting impressions that my thoughts headed off in new directions. I began to remember the happiest times of my childhood: rainy days were the best for my siblings and cousins and for me as well. When we used to ride our bikes, we'd always pass over the puddles at full speed. We loved to see how the water ran and came out like a fountain from the bikes' tires. If we were home, we'd come out to the backyard, get wet while singing and messing around, and we'd run from one corner to the other, sliding at full speed. You don't need to be rich to enjoy and be happy with the gifts of nature.

Back at school, we used to watch the rain fall with our friends. We'd lie down on the floor and close our eyes to enjoy the sound of the falling water. Then when it stopped raining, we'd sit looking at the grass with a refreshment in our hands. We were delighted with the smell left by the passing rain. Going back to my activities in the classroom, I'd bid farewell to the rain and make a wish. All my wishes were fulfilled, some sooner than others, and each one of them, in its best moment, filled my books of memories.

I returned my thoughts to the park and the young man. The frustration and bitterness were still with him, but it was no longer strange to me; it takes a long time for the bad feelings to go away. Unfortunately, it doesn't happen the same way with the good ones.

I was curious to see how much money the young man had collected until then. I stood up from the bench, and I dared to walk to the his case. He seemed to be lost in his thoughts of defeat and, with his mood prevailing, I couldn't feel calm around him. I could only take a quick look. I didn't think I saw any coins or bills, and it was strange. *Maybe he had already collected something and kept it somewhere else,* I thought immediately.

I was close enough that I could see the color of his eyes. They were beautiful, shining like enchanted aquamarine; they were some really charming blue eyes. Without being warned about the spell, I began to admire all of his face: a masculine face with stunning lines; his young skin, without marks, tanned, healthy, and inviting; his mouth, red as a cherry in summer. His dark wavy hair lavishly harmonized with the color of his eyes, mouth, and skin. Although I was marveled, there still were traces of fear and doubt, combined with pleasure. Then I noticed that we were face to face. Naturally, and a bit afraid … I smiled at him while I remembered the thousand times my sister had warned me about not being so trusting because there are good people in this world, but there are very bad people too.

He smiled at me and looked at the sky for a while. Since he kept watching the sky, I turned to look as well, and I saw how the rain was slowly letting up and the sun was coming out again. I stood still, waiting to see what he was going to do. He took his guitar and started playing another song.

This time, he sounded more vigorous, but with less emotion and tenderness. He moved his whole body impetuously, like someone who wants to stand out or attract attention. His music lost prominence, and he became his own protagonist. There wasn't too much difference in the result. Hundreds of people walked from one side of the park to the other and didn't leave any symbol of their appreciation for his performance.

Once again, I didn't understand what he was doing, with so much talent and so many resources, it wasn't necessary to try to go beyond the art itself. It reminded me of those people that, to believe in God, need a miracle or wait for something colossal to happen, like horses of fire, angels flying, rocks falling from the sky, and rivers divided, among other things.

Sadly, I turned my back on him and decided to go back to my duties, but it began to rain again, and this time much stronger than the first time. I hurried into a store, and I could see the young man from there. I was ready to leave the place; I don't know why I turned to look at him once more. The young man took a pack of cigarettes and a lighter out of his jeans and started smoking. His face and body began to look calmer. It seemed as if the young man had finally found some peace. He looked at the case with disappointment, dropped the cigarette, took the guitar and threw it into the case. He kneeled down, took a picture out of the case, and ripped it into many pieces.

I grew tired of watching the young man, so I decided to get closer and talk to him once and for all. The park was full of people even though and the rain was getting much heavier. He took his case and sat next to some resident street people. The crowd started disappearing pretty quickly under the roof of one of the food stores next to where I was. The rain didn't show any signs of stopping soon. Seeing that the weather didn't get any better, I ran as fast as I could to where the young man was sitting, taking for granted that it was fine to sit next to him, so I did. He began to smile, but I pretended that I didn't see him.

My car keys fell from my pocket. He picked them up, and our faces met once more. He smiled and said, "Here. I believe these keys are yours."

"Thanks. You're very kind. I've been listening to you play and sing this morning. Your voice is rich and mellow, and the guitar makes a very good accompaniment."

"Yes, I think the same. Well…," he paused and looked away. "Only you and I believe that. Today, I understood that nobody else believes in my talent or in what I have inside of me."

"Tell me what you have inside. From the distance, I saw two worlds in just seconds. I saw the beautiful, the art, the feelings, the humility, the freedom, the energy, the love, and then I saw the rage, the frustration, the ego, the hatred, the discontent, and the sadness."

"Haven't you experienced something similar in your life?" the young man asked. "You come out to the street to give the best of yourself, and no one acknowledges that, nobody cares about you. I can't change the way others see me. To them, I'm not an artist. To them, I'm just a beggar. I saw you sitting on the bench, and I wondered who you were and what you were doing there for so long. Meanwhile, my frustrations accumulated at seeing that I didn't get anything, and the minutes passed by. Then, to top it off, it rained, and you still were there, as though nothing had happened."

Suddenly, he paused and looked deeply into my eyes. He smiled and said, "Now, I'll play just for you." He took his guitar out of the case and asked. "What would you like to hear?"

I replied, "One of my favorite songs. It doesn't have lyrics, it's only music. I hope you can play it." I laughed aloud. "Hahahahah! It's called *Air in G*, one of the most beautiful compositions by Bach."

The young man nodded his head. "Yes, yes, I know it, but I don't have the music sheet here with me. I've got an idea: I'm going to play a song that I wrote."

I interrupted, surprised. "You write songs, too?"

"Yes, I started writing songs, then I learned to play the guitar, and now I write lyrics and music."

I was even more amazed at this young man. If only he wouldn't let himself be swayed at times, by the negative energies that obscured his understanding and eclipsed his sparkle. I liked his company and the conversation, but suddenly I was concerned that this young man hadn't reached any of his goals during the day, and that it wouldn't be a very good idea for me to become his goal. Meanwhile, he tenderly started playing his song. It was much more beautiful than the others he had been playing before, written by popular singers of the time. I closed my eyes and let the muse take control of my imagination and allowed the tunes to make me go through universes of possibilities in my life. He finished, emphasizing the last string. A tear ran down his cheek, and then I took his cheeks and kissed him. He dropped the guitar and hugged me.

Then I told him, "Yes, it's true. I can see your talent, as well as your desires, and your obstacles as well. How much did you expect to collect today?"

"Well, any amount. I didn't want to have expectations, so I didn't think of a specific amount, but I never thought I wouldn't collect anything at all."

I started looking in my purse, finding a lot of useless things until I finally found forty dollars at the bottom.

"What are you doing?" he asked.

"I'm looking for something for you, and I found it now. Thanks for such a beautiful song, and it is worth more than what I found in my purse. But modestly, it's all I have with me today. I want to ask you a favor before I go."

"Sure."

"Show me how to play your song on your guitar. I promise that each time I play it in my house, I'll say a prayer for you so you can fulfill your dreams." When I finished speaking, I held out my hand with the money.

He saw it, gulped heavily, and took it. His eyes were teary. With a soft, warm voice, he asked, "Who are you? *What* are you?"

I respond eagerly, "Your first fan, perhaps. Believe me, even I don't know who or what I am, or what I'm doing here. Like many others in this world, I'm lost, looking for answers on the river's waters, in the city's winds, the rising sun, the setting sun, the trees that give us shadows.... Now, you appeared today, and an inexplicable force pushed me toward you."

The young man grabbed the guitar and, with amazing patience, began to teach me how to play the song. Time passed very fast while I enjoyed his beauty and talent. I looked at my watch and realized that it was too late, and it had stopped raining completely.

I stood up and said, "Thanks, I have to keep on practicing. Today, both of us have found what we needed. Don't let the obstacles overshadow your senses and make you give up on your destiny. Take control of your anger, impatience, and internal frustrations. The world doesn't owe you anything. Nobody owes you anything; don't do anything to get the approval of others, and don't expect anything in exchange for your good deeds and wishes. Do it all for your joy, to grow up, to take notes and words of love to the universe that saw you being born. What's your name?"

"It's Sam, and yours?"

"It's Julia." I turned around and started walking slowly across the street to my office.

In the distance, I heard Sam's voice. "Wait!" He came closer and said, "Thank you, for everything. My heart only has one more question to ask."

"What is it?" I wondered.

"Will we meet again?"

"Sure we will!"

While I was returning to work, I met two coworkers. We started talking and exchanged opinions about the day. I arrived at my office, sat down in front of the computer, but noticed that it was almost impossible for me to concentrate on my activities. My mind was so distracted by all the memories and sensations experienced in the park. The phone rang, interrupting my thoughts.

"Hello?" I said.

Instantly, an effusive voice asked, "Julia?"

"Yes, this is Julia."

"Julia, this is Alessandra. Are you busy right now, or can you talk?"

"I can talk, tell me."

"I have more good news! Sean proposed to me; we are getting married in a few months. I remembered our dinner together, what you said to me, you were right. He is my true love, I have no doubts." She paused.

"I am so glad for you, Lucas, and Sean. Now, remember that life will test you guys over and over. Don't forget who you are, don't lose yourself, and don't allow any obstacle or challenge to cloud your feelings. I have to let you go now. We should get together and celebrate one more time, talk to you later."

"Okay, talk to you later, have a wonderful day."

"Same." I hung up full of joy; my last mission was definitely over.

Reflecting on everything, I realized that I had finally found my pathway, and it was nothing like I had imagined. It's not about something or someone. The one and only pathway is the way home. I looked through my window, lifted my head with my eyes closed and opened my arms to sky, and through my consciouness, I heard the words:

You have found your pathway...

*　*　*

Julia collapsed at 4:17 PM. A coworker found her and called an ambulance. There was nothing they could do. Julia died of a massive heart attack.

*　*　*

In this life, just like Sam, all of us wish to find somebody who believes in our talent and heart as much as we do, or even more. For sure, Julia will lead the way for this young man, wherever she is.

Will they meet again?

If we open our hearts to hope and the true essence of our existence, the answer to that question would be: YES.

CHAPTER 11

The Messages

THESE WERE THE LAST words taken from Julia's diary, where she wrote down the messages she received days before finding her pathway and happily going home:

There are things that have no explanation, don't have a name, and are not governed by worldly laws. It's difficult for man to believe in them because the way these things are, is completely impossible for the human mind to comprehend. For this, we must silence the mind as a whole, and start seeing through the bright light that flows from the divine creation of every being, and every world, and every space.

Many are trapped in the imagination, which is the proper space for the physical mind, and the true realization and example of the divine world. They are unable to differentiate, and they mistake judgment and truth. Humans constantly have problems understanding some things, because they don't know the nature of those things. Frequently, they talk about the soul, the body, and the spirit. The spirit feeds the soul, and the soul is transported in this earthly world through the body. The body is just the vehicle, although it's just as important in this world as the soul and the spirit are in the healthy spiritual world.

Many times, we see sensitive men or very strong and dominating women, and according to the orthodox bases, they give an impression that it's not fine, or it's not right. What happens in these cases is that we are in a scenario where the body and soul don't correspond from the point of view of the sexuality. That raises much confusion and misunderstanding, combined with the strong and excessive tendency to judge, which is suffered by almost all of mankind.

Therefore, due to the framing by societies and different religions, these individuals tend to suffer too much in life. They spend their lives rejecting themselves instead of accepting themselves, doubting themselves and their own nature, instead of feeling strengthened and walking the way for which they are intended. The spirit has no sex. Therefore, it's an indication of how insignificant sex is, for what we are in essence.

I wonder if there would be any difference or impact in the world if sex wasn't the basis of relationships and marriages, and if understanding, unconditional love, affection, and care were the main virtues, and sex was only a complement. Sex is just the reproductive and biological pleasure path, but it's not the base or fundamental pillar for the cohabitation and longevity of relationships.

Accept yourself just the way you are, a woman with the soul of a woman or man, or a man with the soul of a woman or man, and you'll stop suffering. Peace and tranquility lie in the acceptance of being. At the end of the pathway, who created you accepts you just the way He created you, and you will be standing only before his eyes when you are called.

Although the world has significantly changed with regard to women, their rights, opportunities, values, and roles, we find out that some laws and beliefs about what living as a couple should be, still affect thousands of families.

Another complication that is raised is when the soul has a nature and the mind has a contrary or adverse nature. In this case, you can have methodical, organized, structured, and disciplined mind, but also a free, artistic, expressive, and spontaneous mind. Like an artist trapped in an engineer's mind. This makes the mind and soul divorce in a spot or moment in life, and that divorce leads to the breaking of the spirit and brings out suffering as a consequence.

The possible solution is to find a balance between mind and soul and prioritize the dominance of one or the other based on the environment and situation you currently find yourself in, as well as totally overriding one of them and living life driven and guided just by one of them.

The Pain:

Pain comes to your life once your expectations differ from the way the situations are encountered in your life. Normally, human beings resist everything that is not in alignment with their expectations and wishes. With this, unfortunately, they get away and disconnect from their own selves. They roam among a set of feelings such as frustration, anger, hate, jealousy, envy, etc. It's like an oozing open wound.

Once you accept the moment or situation that you're living in, and acknowledge that life won't always be what you conceive as ideal, then there are many ways, such as God's blessings, which can be irrigated and planted in your life, and you open yourself to all the possibilities and connect with yourself again. The first hint of this is called peace. Peace takes place in the space created for itself, where the fear disappears, and everything around you look harmonious.

You surprise yourself when you see that your wishes are no longer attached to your being. You can live without them, the new representation and the new paths that take place are better and more pleasant, which suits your nature. The only answer to this is that your new paths were created for you specifically by God, while what you wished for in the beginning had been produced by the earthly and material world where you don't belong. But you learn from it, and you overcome yourself to reach higher spiritual levels.

On the side of light, you will live without hate, without jealousy, without selfishness. Sex doesn't matter or exist. Forgiveness is one of the protagonists, and the feelings that you'll find and take over you will be love, affection, and goodness. You'll be free to do what you wish; the wisdom will make you look younger. You'll find the harmony and life in a community, where everyone helps each other.

If you want to return to the earthly world, coming back will be your decision, whether to pay a Karma from your past life, to serve as a guide or protect a relative or a loved one, or to be loved or to carry out some spiritual mission.

Remember that your experiences on the earthly world will lead to the purification of your soul, as well as to the complete loss of it and going back to the spiritual world at lower levels than the one you started from. It's a risk that everyone who reincarnates has to face. It doesn't matter how much you prepare your consciouness. After the first year of life, more or less, the connection with your consciouness will be lost, and you will be left to your own free will.

Most earthlings believe that they must make their own decisions and learn from their mistakes. What they don't know is that all of them, with no exceptions, can get to communicate with their spiritual guides and live their lives under guidance. Even though they don't understand why some things happened in a way they didn't expect, they can trust that, for some reason it was better that way, and move forward in their lives ... guided.

In the spiritual world, you have the power to see the aura and souls of other people, and that is one of the disadvantages of the earthly world, where good and evil are in the same place and we don't have the ability to see them. Now, if you pray and ask our Father to let you see the aura and soul of the people, then He can grant it to you.

THE END

Printed in the United States
By Bookmasters